The Ring of the Seventeen

(Book 3 of the Gate of Fire Series)

B.J. Vanderhoof

Also by B. J. Vanderhoof

The Gate of Fire Series
The Prophecy of the Gate
The Keepers of the Key
The Ring of the Seventeen

Other Stories
Tales from the Kingdom of Tyndall: A Short Story Collection

~ To The Other Sixteen ~
Love You All

THE KINGDOM
Small River Town
Gargan's Clan
SECORD
THE STONE WAY
Bram's Clan
The Gate
Stone Heights
HERITAGE

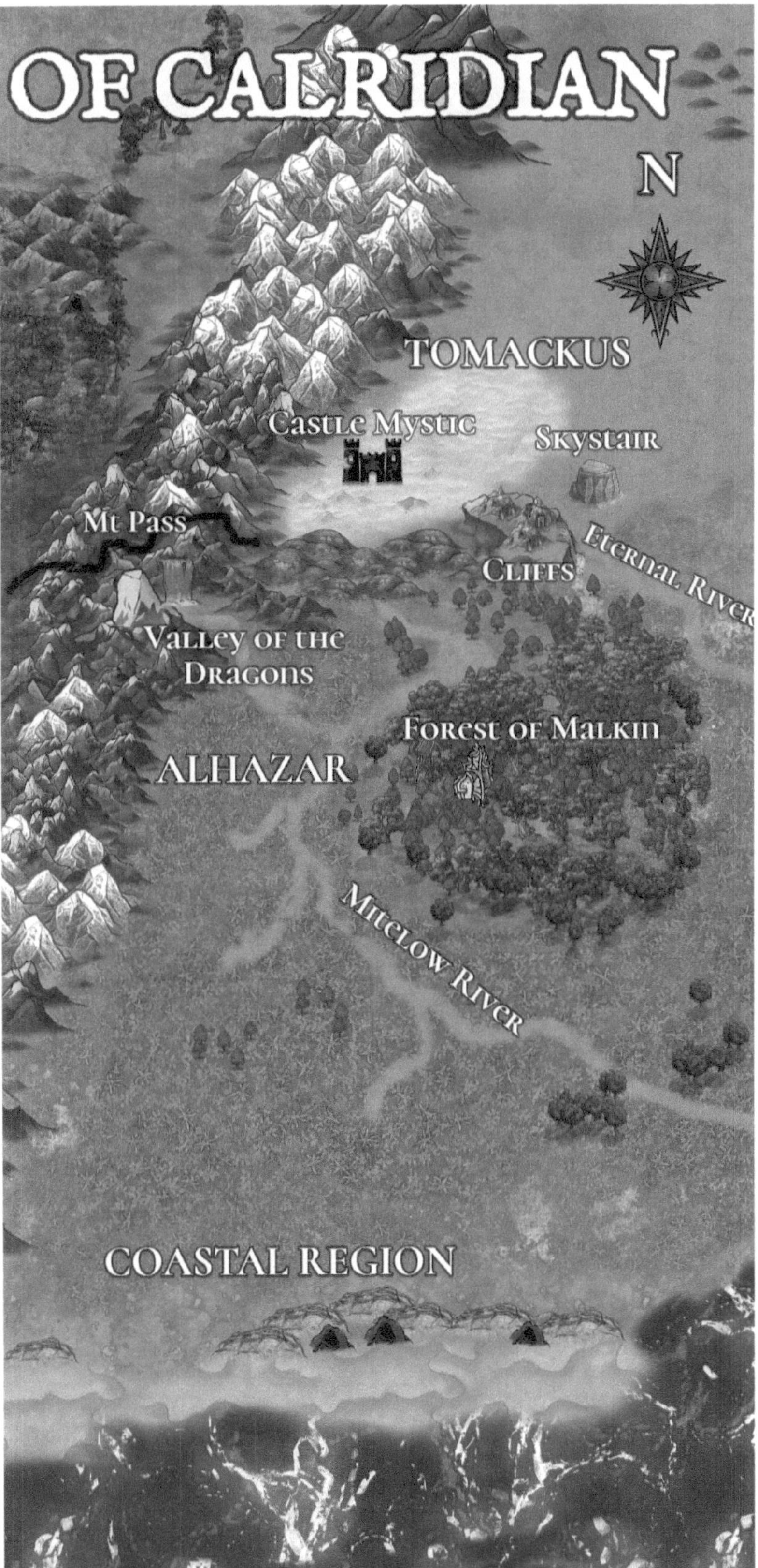

OF CALRIDIAN
N
TOMACKUS
Castle Mystic
Skystair
Mt Pass
CLIFFS
Eternal River
Valley of the Dragons
Forest of Malkin
ALHAZAR
Mitelow River
COASTAL REGION

Characters

The Council of Peace
Malick (*Elf*) - King of Calridian
Esmeralda (*Dragon*) - King's Advisor
Vurth, Son of Rand (*Dwarf*) - Captain of the Guard
Lord Kapel (*Delga*) - Leader of Castle Mystic, Tomackus
Shepherd Rowland (*Human*) - Warden of Skystair, Tomackus
Tagro, Son of Vurth (*Dwarf*) - Dwarven leader, Tomackus
Simamar (*Elf*) - Elven leader, nephew of the King, Alhazar
Ogla (*Orc*) - Leader of the orcs and goblins, Alhazar
Gargan (*Gargoyle*) - Clan leader, The Stone Way
Constance Octavia (*Human*) - Empress of Heritage
Cassie (*Human*) – Representative from Secord
Rutu (*Yixl*) – Representative from the Coastal Region

Roles in the Kingdom of Calridian
Jyres Sands (*Human*) - Former Keeper of the Key
Lalatco (*Elf*) - Former Keeper of the Key
Mit Merrituk (*Human*) - Ambassador
Percy (*Gargoyle*) - One of the King's envoys

Friends of the Kingdom of Calridian
Crimson (*Dragon*) - One of four dragons still in existence
Cyna Sands (*Delga*) - Adopted sister of Jyres
Elonda (*Elf*) - Skilled warrior, from the elven family of Malkin

Hawkins (*Gargoyle*) - Member of Gargan's clan
Kaleido (*Dragon*) - Young Dragon
Leah (*Human*) - Married to Lalatco; Hunter from the Old World
Lumpkin (*Dwarf*) - Dwarven alchemist
Sunbeam (*Dragon*) - Young Dragon

Former Knights of Enchantment
Demorous the Fierce (*Delga*) - Resident of Castle Mystic
Felix (*Delga*) - Resident of Castle Mystic
Sigmon (*Delga*) - Resident of Castle Mystic
Digmon (*Delga*) - Resident of Castle Mystic
The Silver Shadow (*Delga*) - Holder of the key to the Gate of Fire
Bartholomew the Bold (*Delga*) - The Wanderer, Friend of the black donosin
Brigand (*Delga*) - Friend of Karth and the yixl
Karth (*Delga*) - Friend of Brigand and the yixl

Other Characters
Bluey (*Goblin*) - Goblin banished by Ogla
Bram (*Gargoyle*) - Clan leader
The Horde - The reason for the Gate of Fire

Interested to hear how the author pronounces all the characters and places in the Gate of Fire Series? Just scan the qr code.
(You are also free to pronounce them any way you like)

B. J. VANDERHOOF

x

Contents

Prologue

The Making and Unmaking of the Gate of Fire.

The Gate of Fire was made through the crafting of an unbreakable spell made up of power from the triangle, ancient knowledge, a magical item, and precision. The only way it can be undone is through the same way it was made. Here follow the instructions to unmake the Gate of Fire. Be warned, we do not know what will result if the unmaking is successful. Much power would be released. Would the horde survive? Would the Ring of the Seventeen perish? You have been warned.

The spell to create the Gate of Fire required the Ring of the Seventeen. The Seventeen must be spread around the ring of fire equally distanced from each other. The Seventeen are as follows.

Three of each of the triangle

One delga wizard

Six other unique races

The Bear's Heart

The delga wizard must be outside the ring of fire, stationed at the center, facing the front of the gate. One from the triangle must stand next to the wizard. Directly across from the wizard, on the far side of the ring of fire, is where the Bear's Heart must be placed. Two from the triangle must stand on both sides of the item. The remaining triangles are spread equally distanced around the ring of fire, and the other six races are then placed equally distanced in between those of the *triangle. Once the Ring of Seventeen is complete, the spell casting can begin. The Seventeen must hold their positions throughout the entire spell. The spell must be repeated three times, during which the delga wizard must remain fully concentrated in order to be bound with the Seventeen. If all of this is done again in the correct way, the Gate of Fire will be unmade. The spell and diagram follow. Remember, the horde was put there for a reason. The original Seventeen thought it wise to allow the gate to be used via the key. They had condemned the horde to this existence, but had done so in a way that allowed for their decision to be reversed. The creatures can be freed. Or the gate can be unmade. Either way, the world would be changed...*

1

The Questions Remain

After what seemed like the one-hundredth time he had studied it, King Malick put aside the scroll. When Lumpkin had first brought the scroll to him just a few days before, it had seemed like a miracle at the time. The wizard Zar had found the scroll and died shortly thereafter. But it brought more questions than it did answers. What or who was the triangle? What would happen if the Gate of Fire was undone? Did this scroll help them in any way? Zar had somehow seen this as an answer, so he sent Lumpkin to deliver it to the crown as fast as possible. Malick had yet to see what Zar saw in this scroll.

Malick leaned back on his throne and rubbed his hand across his face as if trying to wipe away the tiredness. When was the last time he slept? When Malick wasn't talking about all that had happened, the worries of the recent events prevented him from achieving restful sleep. So much had transpired in the last few days that it was almost too much to comprehend. Jyres was captured. Vurth was unconscious. Zar had died. The Silver Shadow and the horde were now in possession of the key and the Kingdom of Calridian seemed to be doomed before it even had a chance.

Malick breathed deep, let it out in one long exhale, and told himself to relax. Tomorrow would come fast, for he had sent some of his envoys to a select few members of the Council of Peace and requested their presence at a meeting tomorrow. If he was going to lead a productive meeting and start to untangle this web of challenges, he better get some sleep.

The next day came and Esmeralda lay stretched out in the large Throne Room. The room had been built to accommodate the large dragons. To her left sat King Malick on his throne, and across from her was the delga and leader of Castle Mystic, Lord Kapel. Shepherd Rowland was just to the right of Lord Kapel. The king's nephew, Simamar sat across from the king leaving room for one more person in the circle. Gargan, the light green gargoyle entered the room and joined the group, taking the place between Esmerlada and Simamar.

"Welcome, Gargan," said the king. Then addressing the whole group, he continued, "I have called you all here to discuss the scroll that has been delivered to us by Lumpkin, from Zar himself. I know there are many things we could discuss; such as how to go about finding Jyres, or the whereabouts of the Silver Shadow. But let us focus on one thing at a time. So for now, we focus our thoughts and our energy on the knowledge contained in this scroll." Malick reached down and scooped up the scroll from a small table by his side. He then read the scroll aloud for all to hear.

Only Esmeralda and Lord Kapel had heard the letter or even knew of its existence. Gargan's, Simamar's, and Shepherd Rowland's faces reminded Malick of the emotions he had felt when he first read it. In a word…"what?" Knowing how long it took to process everything in the scroll, the king read it one more time before returning it to the table and looking at those seated around the circle.

"This was all that was sent?" questioned Shepherd. "No other instructions or thoughts from Zar?"

"It was just this, and the unfortunate news that Zar is no longer with us. He has passed on." Malick allowed this news to wash over them, knowing Gargan would take it the hardest, as his nephew and Shepherd had not known Zar personally.

Gargan bowed his head and clenched his fists. "This is disheartening news, for he was a friend. And also one who could help us in this time of need."

After a respectful amount of time had passed, the king continued. "Agreed. Which brings us back to this scroll. Zar sent it to us, thinking it would help us. And I believe that it will. We just need to find out how. So, thoughts?"

They all seemed to ponder the matter, not sure what to say.

"Let us begin with one item at a time," said Lord Kapel. "We will start with the Ring of the Seventeen. It states that there are three of each of the triangles. What is the triangle?"

"That is something that I have been unable to discern. As you all know, some of my family of elves have been alive for many, many years. But I have never heard mention of the triangle."

"Yes," mused the dragon, "but remember, the Gate of Fire has been standing untouched for years upon years. It was there before the War of Ages. This is ancient knowledge, ancient power that we are discussing."

"Three of each...to me that seems to say individuals," commented Simamar.

"So, what individuals would make up the triangle?" asked Shepherd.

"Perhaps," started Gargan. Then he paused with his chin tilted up at an angle as if still thinking about his response. "Perhaps the triangle was something much like our Council of Peace."

"I had much the same thought," said Lord Kapel, sitting up straight. "But the writer makes mention of the original seventeen leaving room for their spell to be undone. I assume they would have had the foresight to realize a council or something similar would not be guaranteed to be still in existence. This leads me to believe it is something simpler, but I think that is the right line of thinking."

"A simple triangle," said the king in a soft tone. "Three things. Three things make up a triangle, so three things that could be expected to still be in existence many years after the creation of the gate."

Lord Kapel stood up, and paced the room, before coming to a stop by the circle again. His chin was gripped between his thumb and pointer finger, his expression serious. He dropped his hand away from his face, raising his head and clasping his hands behind his back. "The scroll also talks about six other races. It may be as simple as that three different races represent the triangle."

"Perhaps," commented Shepherd, before pausing to collect his thoughts. "But...but it also says, six other races, right after it mentioned the delga wizard. It could just be a follow-up after mentioning a delga and might not be in reference in any way to the triangle."

"I like this thought, however," said the king. "Let's follow that for now. If it meant three races, which would be part of the triangle?"

"I think it would be safe to say that in the context we have presented, the triangle would be seen as the leaders or powers of their time." Lord Kapel sat back down mid-thought. "As we said, however, this is from an ancient time."

The dragon stretched her neck and said, "I do not doubt your intelligence, my delga friend. But Shepherd makes a good point as well. I would not say it is safe to assume anything. But we have a library. Perhaps that information could be obtained there. Lumpkin and Zar spent a lot of time putting everything in order. It may not be as hard as we fear to find out what the triangle is."

Changing the subject, Simamar asked, "What about the Bear's Heart? Does anyone know what this is referencing? I assume it is not an actual bear's heart."

Lord Kapel chuckled before responding. "No, with the use of the word "the" instead of "a", I think it is safe...sorry, let me rephrase. I think in this case the scroll leads us to conclude it is a reference to an item known as the Bear's Heart. This, too, is unknown to us."

Simamar, the younger elf, had his hands out wide and then shrugged. "Why don't we just look for information on that in the library as well?"

"I would prefer not to put all of our hopes on the library," said the king in a tone that was neither approving nor condescending. "We will certainly have the library at our disposal but there are no guarantees as to what secrets we will find there."

"Aren't we missing the two most obvious issues?" Shepherd ran his hand over his bald head. "I mean, with Zar gone, we don't have a delga wizard anyway." For some reason, that statement, being said out loud in Shepherd's rough-sounding voice, seemed to put a damper on the already desperate conversation. But Shepherd pressed on anyway. "Also, the creators of this infernal gate also have no idea what will happen if we try to reverse the spell."

"I may have a solution for that first issue," Malick said. Only some of the group knew that of which he spoke. "I am not ready to share that yet, so let's focus on the other items first." The conversation turned again to what the Bear's Heart could be. But Malick's mind wandered, thinking of a young delga.

Cyna lay huddled under a blanket. Elonda was sleeping next to her. Elonda had been her rock these last couple of days. Cyna would have been inconsolable without Elonda. Cyna and Jyres had just become a family. They had adopted each other and they had created a family name: Sands. Cyna now had a brother, and anytime she thought about him it brought her to tears.

When Cyna needed to cry, Elonda was there.

When Cyna needed a hug, Elonda was there.

When Cyna needed to scream about the unfairness of it all, Elonda was there.

Cyna pushed her dark hair away from her face and tried to rub the sleep from her eyes. Sitting up, she turned to look at her new friend. Elonda appeared to be fast asleep. As Cyna watched her, she started to realize what anguish the elven warrior must also be in. Here Elonda had been doing everything she could to help Cyna, who felt as though she lost her family, just after she finally had one. But Elonda had lost the love of her life. Cyna maybe didn't know what that felt like, she was a little young for all that mushy stuff. But how Cyna was feeling about the situation allowed her to imagine that Elonda was not in a good state of mind either.

Jyres had been taken by the evil Bram. Elonda had been so sure they would find him in Bram's castle. Only when they went to rescue him, he wasn't there. Bram had hidden him away somewhere, or worse, hurt or killed him. When Elonda returned from her search she was an immediate caregiver for Cyna. As Cyna thought back through the events of the last couple of days, she couldn't even recall Elonda crying. Elonda had been focused on others and had given special attention to Cyna.

Cyna shook her head back and forth. She had been so selfish. No one else would say that she was, or probably even think that. They would say she was a young girl and shouldn't have to experience anything like what had happened to her. It wasn't that long ago that the Silver Shadow held a knife to her throat! But Cyna would not let her age be an excuse. She wasn't the only one who was suffering. Jyres was a dear friend to many. Lalatco, Leah, and Gargan would all be worried about him as well. Plus, on top of that, their other friend, Vurth, was lying unconscious. Cyna shook her head one more time as she let the thoughts tumble around in her mind. Cyna didn't know Vurth very well yet, but she knew enough to understand that the stubborn dwarf was a dear friend to Elonda. So Elonda, in essence, was scared for two of her closest companions right now.

Cyna let out a deep breath before laying back down next to Elonda. Jyres, Elonda, and the others had shown her love that no one else had since she had lost her mother. Now it was her turn to return the favor. Elonda would need her in the coming days, and she would be there for her. Elonda was perhaps one of the fiercest warriors in the kingdom. But even someone like Elonda could only handle so much. She loved Jyres and he was missing and her friend Vurth wasn't doing much better. Time to take the next step. That step? Letting Elonda know that she, herself, was okay and that Elonda would be too.

In the morning, Cyna put on a long-sleeved shirt and walked out of the castle gate. She raised her hands to hold back the brightness from her squinting eyes. After the dark castle, the sunny valley was an adjustment for her. After a few blinks and a few moments, she took in her surroundings. A few people and dwarven guards meandered about. Cyna felt the sun on her, taking away any coolness of the fall morning. Cyna shifted her attention to the middle of the valley where she saw low-flying dragons.

As she walked toward them, she couldn't help but smile. The two young dragons darted to and fro. Sunbeam, the bright yellow dragon, did an inverted circle before landing again with a laugh. Kaleido stayed in the sky a while longer. The sun reflected off its scales, creating a dazzling effect, the orange and blue of Kaleido seemed brighter than ever before.

Kaleido landed with a tumble as Cyna approached. "That wasn't a very good landing," laughed Cyna.

"No, not at all," agreed Sunbeam, whose voice was not like what Cyna had expected when she had first heard her talk. It sounded too close to a female elf, only more high-pitched. "Maybe, I meant to do that," responded Kaleido. Cyna enjoyed hearing Kaleido's voice. She thought it was a calming sound, like the sound of an owl on a quiet night.

"Sure, you did," said Sunbeam before bounding off toward the waterfall at the end of the valley. The two young dragons were always bickering, just like Cyna imagined two young siblings would. Cyna had never had any brothers or sisters until Jyres had adopted her as his sister and seeing the two young dragons together made her miss him all the more.

Cyna stepped up to the male dragon. Cyna enjoyed his company, and he seemed to enjoy hers as well. He was not near as intimidating as the older dragons, as he wasn't even half the size of Crimson or Esmeralda. Reaching out, she patted his head and he leaned into her in return. Leaning against his side she said, "I still don't understand how you can speak the common language already."

"I told you, we just can," said the dragon as he lay down, Cyna matching the movement and leaning against him, now from a sitting position.

"That doesn't really explain it."

Kaleido just replied with, "Okay."

Cyna laughed and yawned before changing the subject. "How far can you fly at one time?"

"I am a dragon," said Kaleido, holding his head high. "So, for as long as I want."

Cyna shook her head. "You make me laugh. You've been alive for a whole week. How do you know how long you can fly without getting tired?"

"I am a dragon," he said again, before rolling on his side, which caused Cyna to lose her balance and bump her head on the ground.

"Hey, warn me next time before you do that," said Cyna as she rubbed her head. "Silly dragon." Cyna fixed her gaze on the mountains that rose up behind Serenity Castle. Somewhere over those mountains, her new brother was waiting for someone to rescue him. She looked over at the colorful dragon, now lying with his back to her. Would he take her to go look for him if she asked? How far could the young one fly and for how long? As she looked at the dragon, she noticed his belly rise and fall in deep, consistent breaths.

"Kaleido, are you sleeping? Really?" Cyna shrugged, whispering, "Silly dragon," under her breath before cuddling next to him. She smiled to herself as she felt her body rise and fall along with the dragon's breathing. As she lay there, she looked down at her hands. Hands that somehow had called the key to the Gate of Fire to their grasp. She reached her right arm out, focusing on a small rock not far from her. Concentrating on that, she said "Stovea." She watched as the rock started to rise off the ground, but it was only for a moment, soon it fell back to the green grass.

Cyna brought her extended hand in front of her face, shaking her head as if it were her hand's fault. Cyna was unsure of what the problem was, but she had struggled to have the same success with the spell that she had had the first couple of times she had used it. And it was not like she knew any other words of power or other spells to try. She also didn't know if she cared or not. Did she want to be a delga wizard? And who would teach her anyway? Zar had passed on, leaving no other option that she was aware of.

Shaking her head again, she nestled back in against Kaleido. So many questions were always assaulting her young mind, and she had no answers to quiet them. As her breathing fell in sync with the young dragon's, her emotions calmed, and she fell asleep, leaving the questions for at least another arc or two.

Elonda took a deep breath and willed herself out of bed. She put on her usual form-fitting dark blue shirt along with her similar-colored pants. With practiced motions, she brushed out her long black hair before pulling it back into a ponytail. The first thing she did was check on Vurth, as had become her habit over the last few days. Vurth had been injured during the battle with the gargoyles and had been unconscious ever since. Others would visit him of course, but few were as faithful in their visits as Elonda.

Vurth was lying on a cot in his quarters. He had been moved there to keep him away from the hustle and bustle of the castle and all the added commotion as it recovered from the battle. Elonda slid into the chair next to the cot. She reached out and grabbed his hand, all the while fearing that one of these times his hand would be cold. She let a small smile grace her face while feeling the warmth of his hand. Elonda shook her head in frustration as she watched her friend's chest rise and fall. *How had this happened* she thought, and not for the first time. But she caught herself, pushing the negativity far away.

As she sat there, not speaking, another female elf entered the room. Elonda nodded to her as the elf checked on her patient.

"Any change?" asked Elonda, already knowing the answer.

"I am afraid not," the other elf replied before stepping out of the room.

Elonda watched her go before turning back to Vurth. "I know you probably can't hear me, but I am going to talk anyway." She leaned forward and sighed before continuing. "Your son has done well in your absence. He has taken over your duties while you recover. But don't worry, I don't think he will have any problems giving them back to you." Elonda stared at her hands for a moment before figuring out what to say next. "The king has been meeting a lot with some of the council, but I don't know what they have all been discussing. There are so many things that need to be done. We need to find the key, we need to stop the Silver Shadow, and we need to find Jyres." Her breath caught, and she paused. "But let's focus on you. We need you. Please wake up." Elonda reached over and squeezed his hand again. She stayed there with her friend for a while longer. "See you later," she finally said.

The next part of Elonda's routine was a morning ride. She tried to stay focused on the next thing, the next task. It seemed to be what kept her sane. Wild Spirit was happy to see his rider and let Elonda know that as soon as she ventured into the stables. He whinnied and tossed his head in acknowledgment. "Good morning," she said as she patted the powerful black horse. She took her time getting him ready, brushing him before saddling him. Her mind drifted back to when she had first tamed the fiery stallion. This thought broke through the straight face she had frozen on her features, and now just the hint of a smile was there. Elonda continued to brush the horse, but Wild Spirit was far from patient, and she could only delay so long. She swung up into the saddle with ease and ushered him out of the stables.

Elonda held Wild Spirit back, taking it slow in the valley. As they moved toward the entrance to the valley, Elonda spied Cyna laying against the dragon Kaleido. Elonda watched them as she went. She was glad the young dragon had taken well to the young delga. Elonda turned Wild Spirit to the west as they left the valley, skirting the mountains. Elonda gave her horse a slight kick and he increased his gate to a trot. Elonda watched the mountains as they went by. Although still tall, this section of the Alhazar mountains was not quite as intimidating as other parts. Elonda let Wild Spirit pick his path forward but kept him at a casual trot.

Sensing Wild Spirit's desire, she leaned down to the horse and whispered. "If we must." Elonda took control of the horse and steered him away from the mountains and into the grass where she gave him another kick and he responded, increasing his rate of speed. Wild Spirit was born to run, and she let him, getting him his exercise. She stayed close to the valley, changing directions when needed and racing across the grassy terrain.

After a while, she slowed him down, allowing him to relax a bit before their ride was over. After an arc's time, she returned to the castle, ready to check her next box on the day's list of activities. She and Cyna had fallen into the habit of helping the stable hands after Wild Spirit's morning ride. Cyna was there waiting for her and together they refilled water and hay for the horses. Cyna had come to enjoy this part of Elonda's routine and her favorite part was helping brush down a few of the horses.

Returning to the interior of the castle they found the kitchen and helped themselves to some bread, cheese, and water. As they ate, they spoke little, each lost in their own thoughts. Cyna, thinking about what she had realized earlier, asked a question or two about Jyres, but Elonda said little in return.

Next on the to-do list for Elonda was to check in with Tagro, the current Captain of the Guard. Tagro, overwhelmed by the tasks needing to be done in place of his father, often took her up on her offers to help. And this day would be no different. She agreed to help him deliver orders to the soldiers of the kingdom, so they knew their roles in the coming days. Orders that told the men and women at arms what arcs they had the watch, or what posts they were to guard, or their training assignments.

After this, her nightly routine would begin. This usually included checking in with the king's guards to see what she could learn from them. One should never underestimate what a soldier so close to the king might hear. That was followed by supper and seeing to anything that Cyna needed. Elonda would then try to sleep, and get frustrated with how long it took to achieve this. She would start all over again the next day. Routine, routine, and denial.

A dark shadowy figure emerges from the trees and walks toward the building at the far end of the beaten bath. He ignores the odd looks, the faces of concern, or the retreating feet of those nearest to him. Some doors on the small buildings that line the path are closed in a panic, others are left open with just the slightest crack from which the inhabitants can watch the unknown figure.

All this the Sliver Shadow sees, but doesn't see. Feels, but doesn't feel. He has one destination in mind and is not interested in the closed doors and startled faces along the path.

The building is a one-story wooden structure with a corner door and a few small windows. Contrasting colors of green and red are painted with no semblance of order across the exterior walls with the words "Slashed Turtle" etched into the wood over the doorway. As he approached the door, the Silver Shadow released the shadows that clung to him, allowing himself to be fully seen. He also pulled back the gray hood and mask that covered him, revealing his angled chin, black and silver streaked hair, and clean-shaven face.

With one smooth motion, the Silver Shadow swung open the wooden door and stepped inside. The smells of beer, sweat, and damp wood assaulted him. The tavern was crowded tonight, and noises of all kinds filled the room. Those nearest the entrance took notice of him but were quick to decide they wanted nothing to do with the stranger. It was not a large area, one main bar was to the left of the entrance with stools next to it. Tables and chairs dominated the rest of the space and left little room for much else. At the back of the room, one board hung from the wall and half-drunk patrons threw knives at the target in the middle.

The Silver Shadow approached the bar, ignoring those he walked by and pretending not to notice the looks these locals gave him. Behind the bar stood a man with a large belly and hands the size of bear paws.

"Hello, stranger," he said as the Silver Shadow approached. "I don't want any trouble here," nodding to the intimidating figure that was the Silver Shadow.

"And none shall you receive. I would like a drink," said the Silver Shadow.

"How do you plan on paying for that? We mostly barter and trade, but if you have any gold, we would take that as well."

"How about a story? I have a tale that will entertain your crowd for half an arc."

"Well, here is the first one," said the big man as he poured a dark thick liquid into a mug. "If your story is any good, you can have another."

Accepting the drink with a nod, the Silver Shadow took a swig. The thick brew was unique, to say the least, but not at all unpleasant. Surprised, he took another drink before standing up tall and calling to those who were gathered.

"Fellow patrons of the Slashed Turtle," shouted the Silver Shadow. "Your attention, if you would." The noise level in the bar decreased as the patrons turned to gaze at the speaker.

Confident that he now had the attention of most of the people, he lowered his voice just a little so he wasn't shouting anymore. "Who here has heard of the elf, Lalatco?" he asked. In reply, he saw a few people nodding and heard a couple of murmurs of confirmation. Continuing on he said, "Very good. And how about the human Jyres?" This brought a more excited response. Most of the patrons were humans, so it made sense that the name Jyres would cause more of a stir.

Smiling, the Silver Shadow said, "Well, what if I told you that I have bested them both in combat?"

"I would say you had too much to drink," yelled one person in the back of the room. This brought laughter to the bar as another human commented, "I suppose you killed a dragon as well?" This jibe caused even more of the patrons to laugh at the man standing in front of them.

But that was okay. The Silver Shadow had them where he wanted them. It also made him wonder if he should tell them that he had killed a dragon way back when, but instead he focused on his original story. "Well, I will tell you what. You listen to my story and then decide for yourself if I am telling the truth." He paused, letting the noise level drop down again in the bar, and took another gulp of his drink. "My name is the Silver Shadow." Any noise that was still evident in the bar dropped away at the hearing of his name. This satisfied the Silver Shadow to no end. His reputation was still intact. Time to increase it exponentially.

"I happen to be in possession of a greatly sought-after item. But this wasn't always the case. In fact, searching for this item is what brought me to confrontation with Jyres and Lalatco. Jyres and I crossed blades first. We happened to come across each other near Heritage. Jyres attacked me for no reason that I was aware of." This was not true, but the listeners didn't need to know that.

"At first, Jyres swung his sword with confidence, but I blocked every swing and every thrust. But I let him continue this fight, knowing I had him after just the first few moments. With ease, I transitioned from defense to offense, and moments later the human Jyres was lying on the ground."

The Silver Shadow paused, letting his words sink in. He couldn't help but smile to himself as he remembered the contest. The duel had been quick and he had proven himself to be the better swordsman. After a sufficient pause and another drink, the Silver Shadow continued his story. "I stood over him for a moment, letting him know he was beaten."

"Why should we believe you?" someone in the crowd questioned.

"Don't believe me?" asked the Silver Shadow with his hands out wide. The Silver Shadow then drew his sword from its sheath and in smooth practiced motions etched his sign on the side of the wooden bar. Two s's next to each other.

"Jyres now wears my mark, proof of my story. But I have one more to tell. Lalatco. Much later the search for this item brought me face to face with the elven warrior Lalatco. Now this, I must admit, I was looking forward to. Who here has not heard of the fighting prowess of that elf?" The question was rhetorical so the Silver Shadow continued. "The elf struck first, and the speed and accuracy of his attacks was impressive. The beginning of the fight was just a sizing up of the opponent as we each learned what type of fighter the other was."

The Silver Shadow reached down and grabbed his mug, finishing the rest in one big gulp. The bartender wasted no time filling up the mug—the story was worth the price.

The former knight continued with his story, telling in detail how the fight continued, stroke for stroke. He could tell that he had his listeners hanging on his every word and got louder and more excited as he neared the end of the story. "Then, Lalatco leaned back as my sword swung at him. Lalatco's body bent back so far that he was almost parallel to the ground. Then he popped back up as my sword went by, just missing him by the thinnest of margins.

Lalatco then scored a hit on me, leaving me bloody." To emphasize the point, the Silver Shadow lifted his shirt to reveal the scar.

The Silver Shadow used the break in the story to take another drink and then continued. "So, you might be thinking that I was in trouble. Well, you would be thinking wrong."

Then the Silver Shadow called the darkness to him and his appearance faded, and before anyone knew what was happening, he was standing behind the person nearest to him. As the darkness retreated from him, the patrons gasped in astonishment. They had never seen anything like it. Most couldn't believe it, even though they had just seen the disappearing act.

Returning to his original position by the bar, the Silver Shadow said, "And before you ask, yes, Lalatco also now carries my mark." The Silver Shadow pointed to the SS on the bar and reached for his mug. After a few big gulps, he returned the mug to the bar. "Thank you," he said to the bartender before turning around and leaving the Slashed Turtle.

Behind him, the bar erupted in conversation. They would be saying things like, can you believe that, or what a story, did you see him just disappear like that? Whether they believed the story or not, was inconsequential. He knew that they would be retelling it either way. And either way, the name of the Silver Shadow would be heard in the back corners of every town. And the name would be respected and feared.

4

Time

Time was a curious thing. And even more so for an elf. They were immortal, age would never claim them. How much time in an elf's life did one year take up? What about a day? A day in the life of an elf was almost insignificant. But right now, to Malick, a day was so important. They needed every arc of every day. And every day that went by was a day closer to destruction. For the key was in the hands of the enemy. And it was only a matter of...time.

Malick walked into the Throne Room and saw most of the members of the Council had already gathered there. A few more of the members had been able to answer the king's urgent message and return to Serenity Castle. So Cassi, the representative from Secord, and Empress Octavia from Heritage were also there in addition to Esmeralda, Gargan, Simamar, Shepherd Rowland, and Lord Kapel. Tagro also took a break from his duties to join the Council in their deliberations.

The king took his place on the throne and took a deep breath. Looking at those gathered, he began. "Time. We are running out of it. And we have much to do. We must decide swiftly and with confidence how to proceed. Many questions lay before us as does the fate of our Kingdom." Malick paused and reached to a table set to the side of the throne and grabbed a parchment he had made a few notes on. "Here is what lies before us."

"The Silver Shadow and the horde have the key to the Gate of Fire.

The gate sits undefended.
Jyres is captured or dead.
There is a way to unmake the gate, but we don't know what the results would be.
We need to know what the triangle is.
We need to know what the Bear's Heart is.
We are all defenseless against the horde except for the yixl."

The room was quiet, with most of the group unsure how to respond. And no one did for some time. Then Cassi, the light-skinned human female from Secord spoke up. She pushed back her short red hair as she spoke. "The towns from Secord are talking about the Silver Shadow. He has visited two towns in the area. In each of them, he talked about his duels and victories over Jyres and Lalatco. He is being talked about all over, and the stories are the same."

"Well, at least we know he is not sitting at the gate," mumbled Tagro.

"Cassi, do we know why he is doing this?" asked the Empress.

"It seems he wants people to know his exploits, his wins. He is bragging about himself," stated the dragon Esmeralda.

Cassi nodded her agreement.

"I would echo those thoughts," said Lord Kapel. "Perhaps we have a little more time than we hoped."

The king remained silent for a moment, wondering if this new revelation on the Silver Shadow did indeed give them the time they needed. Either way, the dangers he had outlined and the questions he had posed had to be addressed. "The gate sits undefended," he said. "I think it is safe to assume that sooner or later the Silver Shadow and the horde will come to the gate. Right now, there is no one to stop them."

"Correct," said Gargan in a low, quiet voice, "but as you said, we are defenseless against them."

"Not all of us," mused Lord Kapel. "Perhaps the yixl are needed."

The king nodded. "Rutu returned to his kind to report what he has seen and heard here in the Kingdom of Calridian. Karth and Brigand went with him. We have just been introduced to the yixl, thus it may be foolish to think they will help us in this. But we have to ask. If there is any way they could help, it must be considered. All in favor of sending a delegation to the yixl, say so now."

Everyone in attendance voiced their support.

The king stood up. "Very well, we have a majority of the Council present and you all agree to this action. I will send Ambassador Merrituk and Elonda to the yixl. Merrituk's skills and Elonda's relationship with the yixl will be our best chance of success." Malick then sat back down.

"King, if I may," said Lord Kapel. "I do suggest we get them there as soon as possible, for as we all know, time is of the essence."

"Crimson can take them to the coast. It is the fastest way," said Esmeralda.

The king nodded. "Yes, I agree." The king looked back at the list in front of him. "Jyres is captured or dead."

Gargan growled, "Why do you speak in such a way? Jyres is alive, and I must free him."

"I do agree, we should free him. But I don't think that is our biggest concern," replied Malick. "The other thi..."

The king was cut off mid-thought by a thunderous reply from Gargan. "I will not hear that! Everything must be undertaken, and saving Jyres shall be done."

For a moment no one said anything, and tension ruled.

Shepherd Rowland was the first to speak and his rough voice cut through the silence. "This is one of our tasks before us. Who will you send to search for Jyres, my King?"

Malick's eyes flicked from one council member to the other. They all watched him, expecting an answer, and recognition came to Malick. They all were in agreement on this. "I assign Gargan, Lalatco, and Leah to this task. They will see it done."

"Agreed," said Gargan, in a tone that Malick would never forget.

The next three lines of notes Malick read together and discussion on the unmaking of the gate, the triangle, and the Bear's Heart began. It was a long discussion with only one plausible solution: to send someone from the Council with Lumpkin to the library. Lumpkin knew those rows of books and scrolls well now. Speed was again the concern and Esmeralda agreed to bring Lumpkin and Cassi to the library.

Elonda was tending to Wild Spirit when a messenger came to fetch her. She left her horse and reported to the king as instructed.

"Elonda, thank you for coming. I have an important assignment for you."

Elonda's face brightened. After so long, it was time. She was being permitted to go search for Jyres.

"You will accompany Mit Merrituk to the yixl. You and he…" But the king was not able to complete the sentence.

"What?" exclaimed Elonda, throwing her hands up in disgust. "Jyres is still out there. I need to be out there right now looking for him."

"I understand your concern. We are sending Gargan, Lalatco, and Leah to look for him. But I need you to talk with the yixl."

Frustrated, Elonda tried not to scream. "What is so important that I need to talk to the yixl?"

"You have already established a relationship with them. And we need their help. They can defend us against the horde."

Elonda had to concede that point. But she still hated it. She wanted to find Jyres. And Mit, why Mit. "I don't need Mit. I can do it alone."

"He is a skilled negotiator, and I think he could be helpful."

"Mit? Are you serious, after what he pulled?"

Malick leveled the warrior elf with a hard stare. "You forget yourself Elonda. You are talking to your king. And I don't know what you are talking about."

Elonda took a deep breath and calmed herself. "Jyres didn't tell you, did he."

"Tell me what?"

"It is not my story to tell. But the point remains the same. I don't need him."

"The orders remain the same," the king answered in a stern tone. "You, Mit, and Crimson will talk with the yixl. Tell them we need their help, and bring them here to help defend the gate."

Knowing there was nothing she could do, she turned on her heels and left the Throne Room. Tears were streaming down her face before she had even taken three steps. She returned to her room and collapsed onto her cot. The tears she had been holding back, denying, all came flooding out. She cried, and cried, for what seemed like arcs on end. She didn't even notice when Cyna entered the room. Cyna laid down next to her and held her close, and the tears kept coming.

When Elonda felt like all her emotion was spent, she stood up, brushed her hair back, and took a deep breath. "Thank you for being there," she said to Cyna. "It should be me comforting you, not the other way around."

"Don't be silly." Cyna got up from the cot and stood in front of Elonda, her head only reaching Elonda's shoulders. "You have been here for me this whole time, and you were hurting just as much as I was."

Elonda hugged the young girl one more time. "The hurting is done, for now. I have a job to do, and I know Lalatco and the others will find Jyres."

"You're right," said Cyna with a firm nod of her head. "They will."

A short time later, Elonda stood in a circle with Cyna, Lalatco, and Leah. Hugging each one in turn and saving Lalatco for last, she looked him in the eyes. "Find him."

"We will, I promise," Lalatco replied before hugging Elonda tight.

The small group looked on as Elonda and Mit walked toward the large dragon, Crimson. "Well, this is going to be an experience," commented Mit.

Elonda did not respond, instead focusing on the magnificent beast before her. "Well, Crimson, I guess we have the honor of a dragon ride. I would be lying if I said I wasn't nervous. Then again, I am all about adventure, and what is more adventurous than this."

"We didn't have time to make it a comfortable ride. Sit between the scales and hold on," replied the dragon.

"That is not very encouraging," whispered Mit under his breath as he and Elonda climbed onto the dragon's legs and then onto his back. Elonda sat near the front of the dragon, trying to get comfortable between the front scales, and Mit was just behind her.

Before they were ready, or had a chance to change their minds, Crimson leaped into the air and beat his wings to gain elevation. Elonda's breath caught as she held on for dear life, almost falling. But it was not long before he was in the air and evened out and she was able to find a comfortable hold. Once she felt more at ease, Elonda was able to fully embrace the new experience and it was like nothing she had ever done. The sun shone bright and reflected off of Crimson, which lit up the sky and clouds around them in a spectacular red glow. She looked forward and to the sides, taking in the vastness of the sky and the dragon's wings. Then, with just a moment of hesitation, she looked down. And far below them were the plains of Alhazar. To be looking down on the kingdom was a thrilling yet gut-clenching sensation.

Elonda returned her attention to the sky in front of her and the dragon's head bobbed with each beat of his wings. Sitting tall in her perch, Elonda put her arms out wide. The wind whipped at her, threatening to dislodge her as her long black hair waved around her. She held that position for another moment, almost screaming in pure exhilaration, but she held it in. The moment reminded her of when she had let Wild Spirit gallop with wild abandon across the plains on their exploration journey. Grabbing the scale again and resuming a more solid seat, she stole a look back at Mit. Mit's face was white, and his whole body was rigid with fear and trepidation as he held on for dear life. She shook her head at him and committed herself to continuing to enjoy this new experience to the fullest.

5
Assignments

Lumpkin's and Cassi's ride with a dragon did not go quite the same as Elonda's and Mit's. Esmeralda had tried to be patient with her two passengers, but as neither seemed all that keen on climbing on the emerald-colored dragon, she took matters into her own hands. She scooped them up, one in each of her front talons. Out of sheer nervousness, Lumpkin couldn't stop stammering on about all sorts of nonsense. Cassi, to her disappointment, screamed for the first part of the journey. Once they both settled down, Esmeralda offered an apology.

"I am sorry for frightening you. Dragons have never been known to be patient. I often forget that races such as yours were not made to be in the sky. But do not worry, you are safe."

"Ground better," Lumpkin said in a tone that left little room for doubt. "Wind, cold."

"I tend to agree with the dwarf," snickered Cassi. "I think you are right Esmeralda. We were not made for this."

Upon reaching their destination, the library of Secord, Esmeralda waited outside as Cassi and Lumpkin headed in to begin their search for any information on the triangle, the Bear's Heart, or the unmaking of the gate. Esmeralda didn't pretend that it wouldn't be a long wait, but it couldn't be helped, as there was no way she would fit in the underground library anyway. But a dragon never passed up on an opportune moment for a nap.

Lumpkin led Cassi down the steps and into the great hall of the library. Flashes of memory came flooding back to Lumpkin as he remembered coming here for the first time and seeing the wizard, Zar. Lumpkin smiled as he thought of the old man and the time they had spent with each other before Zar had passed on from this world. Cassi, on the other hand, was experiencing this for the first time. Very little had surprised her in her young life. Today, however, was a different story. First, a ride in a dragon's grip, dangling over the land. And now an underground, yet magnificent, library.

"Here, we begin, begin here," said Lumpkin pointing at a section of books.

Cassi, who didn't stand much taller than the dwarf, nodded her head. "What am I looking for?"

"History. These books, books written in Secord, history."

"History, okay, got it, I think." Cassi reached out and plucked an old leather book from the shelf. "Here we go."

A few arcs later neither she nor Lumpkin had had much success, Lumpkin had found one reference to the triangle, but it didn't reveal anything helpful on what the triangle was. Cassi had not found what they were looking for but learned a lot about the library, how it was organized, and about the wizard, Zar. Lumpkin liked to talk, and she didn't mind listening to him. It was obvious he had grown fond of the wizard during their time together.

After coming up empty with the Secord history section they moved to a different section of the library. These shelves held records that were written in the region around Heritage, back when that area had several towns near the great city. Lumpkin had thought that this would be the second best place to look. Cassi returned the current bound journal she was inspecting to the shelves and picked up another one. This one was titled with the word "Antiquity." Another in the long list of books she was going to have to look at. As she sat down and opened the book, Cassi wondered if Elonda and Mit were having any more success than she and Lumpkin.

After the exhilarating ride on the back of a dragon and a quick reunion with Rutu, Elonda took the time available to rest, as did Mit. The morning would bring talks and the urgent request for help from the yixl. A request that she had not talked over with Mit yet. She had no trust in him and preferred he let her do the talking, a thought she was going to share with him as soon as they awoke.

When the morning came, Mit didn't take to Elonda's suggestion very well. This didn't surprise Elonda in the slightest. "The king assigned me to this task whether you like it or not. So I am here and will see it done."

"See it done," scoffed Elonda. "No matter what. Right? No matter who you hurt along the way."

"So, that's what this is about, I formed an alliance with Heritage. Jyres was my way of doing that." Mit's arms were growing animated and his voice was rising.

"Of course, that is what this is about," screamed Elonda. "I can't trust you, nor will I. I can work with the yixl without your interference."

"Listen. I did what was needed. It is done. Let's focus on saving the kingdom, shall we?"

"Just that easy, huh? Move on, no problem?"

"The Kingdom of Calridian is what matters." A more calm Mit smiled.

"And your place in it," huffed Elonda. "Just let me do the talking, it will go better for everyone." Elonda turned on her heels and left their small cave on her way to the audience with the yixl leader.

Mit followed at what he hoped was a safe distance.

Elonda and Mit entered the large cave with the raised stones in the middle. Torches were attached to the walls and lit in a pattern of every other, offering a small yellow glow. The leader of the yixl stood on the raised stones and Rutu was not far from him. The former knights, Brigand and Karth, stood in front of the stones and Elonda and Mit were led by two yixl to stand alongside the former knights.

"Good to see you, Elonda," said Karth.

Elonda nodded and looked at the leader. The leader stood with that bend to his posture all yixl seemed to have. A smile came to his lizard-like face before speaking in his click-clack language.

Karth turned to Elonda. "He welcomes you back to his cave and says your beast has scared his people."

"Thank you for your welcome. I do realize that the dragons can be intimidating creatures, but I promise he will not harm any of you," replied Elonda, looking at the yixl leader as Karth translated.

The leader responded and Karth again was talking to Elonda. "He asks why you have come so quickly, for Rutu has just returned from his journey with you to your kingdom."

"Yes," Elonda started. "I do realize we were not expected this soon. But time is critically important right now."

"Why?"

Before Elonda could respond, Mit jumped in. "We are here to humbly ask for your help. Our kingdom is in grave danger."

The yixl leader turned to talk to Rutu before speaking again to Karth, who continued his translations. "He asks who it is that speaks now."

"I am Ambassador Merrituk," said Mit, stepping forward. "I come from the king himself with an urgent request." With a nod from the leader, Mit continued. "Our kingdom is in danger from the creature known as the horde. I assume Rutu has told you about this creature. It seems yixl have a natural defense ability against the creature, something no one else has." Mit paused, giving Karth time to translate before continuing. Elonda stood boiling in frustration next to him. "We would ask the yixl to consider helping us against this creature, or our kingdom may fall."

After hearing this the yixl leader began conversations with those around him, including Rutu. As the conversations took place, Elonda and Mit waited. "What are they saying?" asked Elonda. The question was directed at Karth.

"They are talking fast, so it is hard to distinguish everything but some are asking why they would be asked this, and others are wondering how they could be helpful when you have flying beasts. Rutu has been asked questions directly as well."

After a few more moments the leader turned back to them and spoke at length in his click-clacking style.

"To paraphrase," Karth said, "They want to know why they should risk their kind in this battle you have with the creature."

This time Elonda beat Mit to the punch. "Because..." she started, before turning to look at Rutu. "No, you shouldn't."

Mit threw his hands up in defense, "What?" he yelled.

Elonda ignored him. "As a leader of your people, this is not a fight you need to send them to. But I am not asking for help from a leader. I have learned that the power of friendship can conquer all. I am asking my friends for help. Rutu already saved me once by putting himself between me and the horde. I would ask if he would consider helping me again."

Mit was frustrated beyond belief. "What are you doing?" he whispered to her. "I was already making progress. Now what have you done?"

"I spoke the truth, something that maybe you are not used to doing," Elonda shot back.

After more conversations, Rutu was the one to speak this time and Karth translated.

"The leader has granted me permission to ask for volunteers from our warriors to accompany me in my wish to help you. We will be going with you as friends, not officially from the yixl, but also knowing full well that your enemy could also become our enemy."

Elonda turned to face Mit. "Anything else to say?" she asked before running over to hug Rutu.

For some reason, Calli had a good feeling about this book she was reading. Although she hadn't yet found an answer to any of their questions, she felt as though she was getting closer with this book, *Antiquity*. Lumpkin had quieted as of late, but whether he needed a break from talking or thought he was on to something, as well, she could not say.

A few pages later it happened. "Lumpkin," she cried at almost the same time he said, "Look, look." It seemed they both had stumbled across something. Lumpkin brought his book over to where she was reading. "Listen," she said, pointing to a line in the book as she spoke. "The triangle, a reference to the three powers of our time, began most years with a proclamation of what the year would bring." Cassi looked over to Lumpkin who was now jumping up and down in excitement.

"My turn, my turn," he said. He looked down at the book in his hands and was careful to pronounce each word as he read. As he read what was written his cadence was now more normal, and it seemed almost wrong coming from him. But the words themselves were what was important. "The leaders of the current age, the dragons, the delga, and the black donosin were often referenced together as one."

"We found it! Yes! Found it! Triangle," Lumpkin stammered. The next three words they said together. "Dragon, delga, donison."

6

Lost But Not Forgotten

Although Leah and Lalatco didn't have a dragon to ride, with Gargan and a few gargoyles they still were happy with the amount of time it took to cross the mountains and enter the region known as the Stone Way. Along the way, Gargan had explained that even though the king was not immediate in giving any specific orders, Gargan's clan of gargoyles had been watching and tracking Bram's clan of gargoyles ever since they had captured Jyres. Although this had not yet produced the precise location of Jyres, they believed they were starting to narrow down the options.

Right after Jyres had been taken, Elonda and Tagro had searched Bram's castle while the gargoyles were in their stone slumber but were devastated to find he was not there. Now, a few days later, the search continued. Though, if Gargan was right about their progress, having fewer possible spots to check than what Lalatco had envisioned was a good thing.

"Where do we start then?" asked Leah.

"I do not know for sure," replied Gargan. The large gargoyle kneeled on the ground, one large hand cupping his chin. "Though I do have one idea."

"Let's hear it." Lalatco nodded and kneeled as well, anxious to hear what Gargan had to say.

"My thought is to bring my clan against Bram's. And to let him know I am coming."

"How does that help us?" asked Leah, joining the others on one knee.

"If he knows I am coming," continued Gargan, his face set, his voice rumbling from somewhere deep within, "he will keep almost all his gargoyles home, meaning the few that aren't at his castle will be much easier to track."

"So, Leah and I follow those that aren't at the castle, and hopefully it leads to Jyres. A solid plan," thought Lalatco.

"A few of my gargoyles can help you as well."

"But what about you Gargan," said a concerned Leah. "That would put you and your gargoyles at risk."

Gargan smiled. "It is time."

Two nights later, after Gargan had spent the night in between planting seeds that they were coming to confront Bram, Leah and Lalatco waited by some hills a little southwest of Bram's castle. There they awaited any news from Gargan's gargoyles. That night, Gargan had hoped the majority of Bram's clan stayed close to the castle. This meant his gargoyles assigned to tracking the movements of the enemy had a much more manageable job.

It was hard to wait but they waited, knowing Jyres was out there somewhere and knowing Gargan was putting himself in harm's way. They passed the time in each other's company. A love had grown between Lalatco and Leah that no one could measure. And neither one of them would want to spend the challenging waiting time without the other.

Not long after sundown, when the night moon began to shine and the gargoyles had awakened from their slumber, Gargan called to his brethren.

"The time is upon us," he called as his gargoyles climbed, flew, or glided to where he stood at the top of their castle. "Bram has always been opposed to us. We have all felt his anger, his wrath. No more. The time has come. Tonight we confront that which has plagued us. Rise with me. We take to the sky, we ride the wind. Let it take us to our enemy." Gargan then leaped into the air, unfurling his wings and rising on the wind. Over a hundred gargoyles joined him. The sky was full of gargoyles of every shape and size. Some flying, some gliding, some who had neither the ability to fly nor glide being carried by those that did. All of them were following their leader, and all of them were just as determined as he.

They went straight to the south, going on a direct route toward Bram's castle. As they went, a forest was to their east. This was the forest where Jyres and Lalatco had first met both Leah and later Zar. They continued on past the forest, which led them right to their intended destination. As they soared over swampy terrain the castle came into view. Many gargoyles could be seen in the skies above the castle.

Gargan slowed and brought his clan in an arc skirting the lake below them. Calling out to the enemy he yelled, his voice carrying on the wind. "Bram, in the ways of old, I ask for a stone parlay, to address what is before us."

A path in the sky opened up to him, Bram's gargoyles clearing the way. Gargan and two others soared through it landing next to Bram and two of his gargoyles at the top of his castle. "You have your stone parlay, speak quickly," said the big purple gargoyle.

"I give you the opportunity to stand down," replied Gargan with a wave of his hand.

A deep laugh rumbled through Bram. "And why would I do that?"

"To save your clan from the battle that will take place otherwise."

"You came here, Gargan, you have brought your clan, this is your doing. Don't pretend that it is I who started this battle."

"No, but you started the war. I intend to end it," Gargan said in a way that was so matter-of-fact that it was almost boastful. Like the end was a forgone conclusion.

"Leave and ready your clan, before I kill you where you stand. The stone parlay is at an end," Bram sneered.

Gargan and his two fellow gargoyles retreated as fast as they could and joined their comrades in the sky. "We have come to it," bellowed Gargan, the green gargoyle making sure all of his clan could hear him. "Show them what it means to be a gargoyle from Gargan's clan."

That was all Gargan had time to say. Bram's gargoyles attacked, and chaos reigned.

Even from this far out, you could not miss the swarm of shapes above the distant castle. All Lalatco and Leah could do was look on and wait. Both wondered what was happening and how Gargan's clan was fairing. But perhaps it was for the best that they didn't have time to let their minds wander, for a gargoyle landed nearby, and it was out of breath.

"Old. Castle. Jyres," the small gargoyle spat out as it pointed off to the south.

The gargoyle didn't have a strong command of the common language, but its message was clear. Lalatco and Leah both looked in the direction the gargoyle pointed. "Stone Heights," they said in unison.

"It will take a couple of days to get there from here, but we must go as fast as we can," said Leah in a hurried tone.

"Perhaps, we can get some help with that." Lalatco motioned to the gargoyle and with a few basic words hoped the gargoyle got the message.

The gargoyle, seeming to understand, took flight, flapping its wings to speed away. It was not long before it returned with two other, bigger gargoyles. Wordlessly, Leah and Lalatco each climbed on the back of one of the bigger gargoyles and they flew off to the south.

Jyres sat in his cell. The cell in the ruins of Castle Stone Heights was cold, dark, and damp. There had been a change, though, in the last couple of days. Along with the once-a-night visit from a gargoyle who delivered just enough food and water for Jyres to survive, eight other creatures now guarded the cell as well. Jyres had never seen these kinds of creatures before. They were all about the height of dwarves, perhaps a bit taller. They had orange-colored fur with patches of brown all over their arms and legs. Their torso had less fur and what looked like a hard brown exterior. Each of them carried a spear that was a little longer than they were.

Jyres had decided that either the creatures didn't speak the common language or just chose to ignore their prisoner. The few times he tried to talk with them, they didn't even so much as glance in his direction. Jyres was also unsure of why the change had occurred, and why he was now guarded day and night. He hoped it meant his friends were close to finding him. The only knowledge he had of the passage of time was when he received his water and food at night. He knew another day had gone by based only on that. His small dinner was also the only thing he had to look forward to. With no one to talk to, and no hope of escape, what else was there to do?

Early on in his imprisonment, he had tried plenty of things to break out of the cell. But it was no use. He had only been let out of his cell on a few occasions and it was at random times. Nothing Jyres could plan for. The only thing in his cell at a given time was a chamber pot, a tin plate, and a cup. Nothing that could aid his escape in any way.

He had already been fed on this night, and two gargoyles had just left, leaving the eight creatures who milled about in the dungeon. They looked to be just as bored as he was. Jyres put his head against the back wall of the cell and closed his eyes. His only way to keep himself sane; thinking of his friends, his adopted sister, and his Elonda.

His thoughts drifted to memories as he fell into a light sleep. He remembered being with Elonda by the waterfall in the valley, and smiled at the time when he was drinking with Vurth and the others in the tents before the completion of Castle Serenity. Lalatco and Leah sprang to mind as he remembered their wedding and heard their voices.

7

Castle Serenity

Both Esmeralda and Crimson returned along with their passengers to the delight of everyone, including Kaleido and Sunbeam. The two young dragons ran around the older dragons, playing, jumping, and bumping into each other. Cyna was there with the young dragons and enjoyed the scene. Likening it to how young children would play with their parents after being apart.

Elonda was pleased to see Cyna and swallowed her in a hug. "How are you? Everything okay?"

"Yes, Elonda, I am fine. What about you? Will the yixl help us?" asked Cyna.

"Yes, they will. Rutu and some of their warriors are on the way, it will just take a little while without a dragon to ride on. But there is no way the yixl would agree to that, even if we wanted them to." Elonda paused, lowering her head, and in a quiet nervous voice asked, "Any word about Jyres?"

"No, sorry, nothing yet. But he will be okay, I just know it," replied Cyna trying to convince herself as much as Elonda.

Elonda patted her on the shoulder as they and everyone else made their way inside the castle.

After hearing all of the reports, the king gathered those members of the Council of Peace who were present at the castle together in the Throne Room. That included Esmeralda, Tagro, Cassi, the Empress of Heritage, Shepherd Rowland, Simamar and

Lord Kapel. King Malick started the meeting by reading the same list he had read the last time they were together.

"The Silver Shadow and the horde have the key to the Gate of Fire.

The gate sits undefended.

Jyres is captured or dead.

There is a way to unmake the gate, but we don't know what the results would be.

We need to know what the triangle is.

We need to know what the Bear's Heart is.

We are all defenseless against the horde except for the yixl."

Malick paused before adding, "the yixl are on the way here, though it will take some time for them to get here. But perhaps they can help us defend the gate. Gargan, Lalatco, and Leah are looking for Jyres as we speak. We also now know what the triangle is. The triangle is close to what some of you had guessed. Three races represent the triangle. Dragons, delga, and the black donosin."

"And we know that the ring of the seventeen requires three of each of the triangle," Simamar reminded everyone.

"Correct," replied Shepherd. "This is good news. For we know more than three delga, and now have four dragons. And, there are most likely many more than three black donosin."

"Which delga and dragons would we want to use?" asked the Empress."

I don't think we need to focus on the who just yet," replied Malick, "Remember, we don't even know if we want to unmake the gate."

"Were you able to find anything else at the library?" asked Tagro in a tired voice. He had just been sitting with his father, and fell asleep there. He directed his question to Cassi and the council members turned toward her.

"Unfortunately, we didn't find anything else about what would happen at the gate if the Ring of Seventeen were used, or anything about the Bear's Heart. But we thought it important to get the news of the triangle back to the Council, and Esmeralda agreed."

"It was the right decision," said Malick. "We are making progress on our tasks. We must continue that progress. Until the yixl arrive, I suggest we defend the gate the best we can."

"How do we do that?" asked Simamar.

Esmeralda lifted her head. "The dragons have not been tested against this creature yet, Crimson and I can stand guard at the gate. Its powers may not hold any sway over us."

"Although a risk, I agree, it is the logical decision," said Lord Kapel. And others assented as well.

"Very well." The king nodded. "I also think it is important to talk with the black donosin as we may need at least three of them. We will need to find the Wanderer." The members of the council shook their heads in agreement before the king continued. "We are still receiving reports that the Silver Shadow continues to flaunt his name and his deeds to the small towns, but I am afraid that he will have finished that soon."

"We will continue to do all we can to fight against these odds stacked against us. Every time we take a step forward, the odds improve. Keep taking steps, it is all we can do." After saying that, Tagro sat up and left the group, intent on returning to his father's side.

The others dispersed as well, each to their own task or temporary quarters in the castle.

Tagro entered his father's quarters, shutting the door behind him before looking up. To his absolute shock, his father Vurth was sitting up in bed! His eyes open with a look of bewilderment on his face.

"Father!" Tagro cried. "You're awake."

"Well, why wouldn't I be, the sun is out is it not?" replied Vurth, seeming confused by his son's antics.

"How do you feel?"

"I am fine. What's wrong with you? Asking questions like that."

"Dad, you have been unconscious for days, so I am sorry if my questions are a little irritating, but you can understand the concern."

Vurth looked at his son for a long moment, before looking himself up and down. "Well, I'll be dipped," said the grizzled dwarf as he stroked his beard.

"What?" was all the younger dwarf could think to say.

"Well, kiss ol' Rose."

"What are you talking about?" yelled the irritated Tagro.

"I guess you will still be keeping the name Tagro, son of Vurth, after all. Haven't outdone me quite yet." Vurth paused, one hand scratching at the side of his face. "Last I remember, I was in a battle with those gargoyles, and took a blow to the head, I guess. And you say that was many days ago?"

Tagro nodded in return.

"Huh. Well, I am still here. What did I miss?"

Tagro first fetched the elf who had been seeing to the care of Vurth. After the elf looked him over and asked him a few questions, she was amazed at his condition. But she asked Vurth to take it easy for a while and she left the room, leaving father and son alone. Tagro then filled Vurth in on everything that had taken place since the battle with the gargoyles. Vurth let his son tell the tale and didn't interrupt except to ask a question here or there. Often, he just nodded and motioned for Tagro to continue. When Tagro was done, Vurth gave a final nod and started to stand up. He was immediately dizzy, and Tagro helped him sit back down.

"Maybe that elf was on to something. I think I will stay here for a little while yet. But don't go off saving the kingdom without me."

Tagro just shook his head at the stubborn dwarf before heading off to spread the good news that Vurth was alive and well, more or less.

Lumpkin had graciously accepted the king's offer for him to stay at the castle for a while. For his part, he was kind of lost as to what to do next. When he had first sought out the library of Secord he had been looking for ways to increase his ability to produce potions. Although he was able to do that to some extent, helping Zar organize and catalog the library became the priority. With Zar now gone, going back to the library seemed...lonely. He didn't want to sit in that big old library all by himself. So here he was at Castle Serenity.

To pass the time, he found himself spending a lot of time with Cyna and the two young dragons. These dragons were not as frightening as the older ones. He remembered when they came and took his dragon pericarp from him. He had hidden behind Zar. But that same fear was not present with Sunbeam and Kaleido. Lumpkin walked out of the castle and followed the river toward the waterfall as he continued his line of thinking. Although the size was certainly a factor, Lumpkin thought his positive outlook toward the young dragons was driven more by their carefree nature. Ironic that, as he had that thought, he spotted Kaleido running through the valley with Cyna on his back. Sunbeam flew over them, cheering them on. All three were laughing as they went along until Cyna lost her hold and tumbled to the ground. This brought the dragons to a halt. As they were quick to come to Cyna's side, Cyna sat up and had leaves and grass sticking to her frizzy hair. Both dragons started to laugh. Soon Cyna joined them and all three were rolling around the ground in uncontrollable laughter.

Lumpkin smiled at the sight, increasing his walk to a jog and heading in their direction. By the time he had joined their small circle, they had composed themselves.

"Hey, Lumpkin," said a still-smiling Cyna. "Want to ride a dragon?"

"Me? Fall. I would fall. Sooner, I think, than you," said Lumpkin with a shrug.

Sunbeam, lying on her back with her legs up in the air, looked over at the dwarf. "Lumpkin, what kind of name is Lumpkin? It's so funny."

"Um, name, um it's my name. Lumpkin son of Lustor," mumbled Lumpkin.

"Ignore her." Kaleido laughed. "She doesn't like anybody's name unless it is something with the color yellow."

"Not true," said the yellow dragon. "You take that back. I like plenty of names."

"Yes, like Sunflower, and Sunny, and Gold, um...oh and..." But Kaleido did not get to say any more names. Sunbeam plowed into him and the two dragons snapped at each other and pushed the other one to the ground as soon as they had regained their balance.

Lumpkin and Cyna could not help but laugh at the dragons' antics. After a few more moments Kaleido leaped in the air to get away from his tormentor, but Sunbeam followed.

Lumpkin and Cyna sat in peaceful quiet for a while before Cyna said, "Do you miss the library, Lumpkin?"

"Zar," the dwarf replied. "Miss Zar."

"Oh. I know what it is like to miss someone." Quiet fell between them again until Cyna asked, "Hey, you do magic right?"

Lumpkin nodded.

"Have you ever had a spell or something that, for some reason, just didn't work anymore? You know, like something you did worked great, and then all of a sudden it just stopped doing what you wanted it to do?"

Lumpkin had to think about that for a moment. He had made potions that simply didn't work. But had he made one that worked the first time, only to not work the next? He sat scratching his cheek while he thought. Then he had it. Lumpkin bounced a little on the ground before turning to Cyna. "Once I made a potion, potion once that worked, but worked only once."

"Okay, great. Sorry, not great for you, but, oh—you know what I mean. What happened?" asked a curious Cyna.

"Looked at the ingredients. I looked. Made another potion and tried again. Tried again many times."

"Well, did it work how it was supposed to?"

"Yes, well…yes it did. Worked, yes."

"How did you get it to work?"

Lumpkin had to think about that one again. How did he get it to work? He was puzzled for a few moments and then said, "Tried. Just kept."

"You just kept trying, got it."

"Well, I guess that is about all I can do anyway." Cyna let out a deep breath. It was not the answer she was hoping for. But at least it was an answer.

S warms of gargoyles collided in the sky. Fights raged there as well as on the castle walls. Gargan swooped under an enemy gargoyle before being batted aside by another. Gargan was quick to recover and allowed the wind to float him toward another target. He drew his arm back and punched the Bram follower in the gut. The enemy doubled over, losing its control in the air and falling away. Gargan opened his wings a bit more and the wind lifted him over the next gargoyle and then Gargan shot forward. He threw his shoulder into another enemy, knocking it off its path.

With no immediate enemy, Gargan surveyed the scene as his clan continued to battle on. It was hard to distinguish whose side was winning. Killing or severely injuring a gargoyle was no easy task, as Jyres and his friends had discovered on a few occasions. But this time, it was gargoyle against gargoyle. Beast against beast. Strength against strength. Only time would tell which side would prove the stronger. But Gargan knew he could shorten the fight and lessen the number of casualties by defeating the leader. Bram. Gargan scanned the area looking for him. He swept his eyes around a second time before he spotted him near the castle.

The sheer number of gargoyles in the sky was going to make it difficult to get to Bram. One thing at a time. Gargan made progress toward the castle by defeating one gargoyle after an-other, removing them from the battlefield either temporarily or permanently. An attacker's punch grazed Gargan's shoulder but didn't do enough to knock Gargan off his path. He continued to glide forward, dodging, or using force to clear his way.

The battle now ranged all over, with gargoyles fighting on the ground, in the castle, and in the air. As the clans fought, more distance was put between the combatants as they flew or glided around the area, avoiding or chasing attackers. A few gargoyles from each clan had already lost their lives, either by falling from the sky and dying on impact or via the pure strength of their enemy.

Bram landed on the castle wall and ducked under a swooping enemy. He charged a fierce-looking gargoyle, plowing into him. The short fight ended with the enemy lying motionless on the wall. Bram smiled a wicked smile before turning his attention back to the sky to look for his next combatant. Bram saw Gargan and focused in on him. He was making his way to the castle, and Bram would be waiting for him.

Gargan landed with a crunch and Bram did not give him any time to react. Bram attacked. He landed a punch across Gargan's face. But Gargan blocked the second punch with his left arm, before bringing his right fist into Bram's midsection. Bram staggered back a step, smiled, and launched another attack. Gargan only half dodged it and they collided with each other, falling to the stone floor. Gargan pushed Bram over the ledge and the purple gargoyle fell towards the inner courtyard of the castle.

Gargan watched as Bram unfurled his wings, slowed his descent, and landed without issue on the ground. Gargan was about to jump and follow him but two others from Bram's clan surprised him, jumping on him and holding him down. Gargan struggled against the weight and strength of his attackers, grunting under the strain. He let out a battle yell as he shoved the one on his right off him just enough to then focus all his strength to his left and push the enemy away. Gargan didn't give them time to react and jumped straight into the air.

He was only in the air a moment before a gargoyle flew into him at full speed and they both started to tumble out of the sky. Gargan recovered from his haphazard fall in time to avoid slamming into the ground. Safe on the ground now, he surveyed the area for Bram. He spotted him, on the far side of the courtyard, battling with another of Gargan's clan.

Gargan charged in that direction, batting aside one gargoyle who thought he could get in his way. Bram turned to see Gargan's charge. And they both smiled. Bram thought he had gotten under the skin of Gargan, and Gargan was thinking this battle between them had reached an end.

Bram met Gargan's charge, and gave up little ground as their arms locked in front of them, each pushing the other with their brute strength. Their well-defined muscles strained against the other, neither one gaining any advantage. Then Bram broke his hold and thrust a knee into Gargan's midsection, which Bram followed up with an elbow on his back, forcing Gargan to the ground. Gargan was quick to roll to his left as a punch from Bram struck the ground in the spot Gargan had just vacated. Gargan regained his footing in time to dodge another punch from Bram. Bram's reward was to be tackled to the floor.

The two big gargoyles' battle of strength continued. Each of them landed numerous punches on the other and neither gained a significant advantage, leading to the two of them being locked in a fierce embrace again.

"You will not win," grunted Bram. Gargan did not respond and Bram yelled at him this time. "You hear me, you will not win!" Bram twisted and pulled with all his strength, somehow moving the big green gargoyle and pinning him against the castle wall. A large smile spread across Bram's face as he forced one arm right under

Gargan's chin and pressed it against Gargan's neck. "See, I will win!" Screamed Bram, his voice fierce and his face locked in an intense stare.

"Not, quite, yet," Gargan managed to say as Bram's arm started to crush his throat.

Bram still had one of Gargan's arms pinned, but Gargan's free arm slammed into the side of Bram's head. Bram was able to maintain his position through the first blow, but the second knocked him aside and Gargan used the moment to struggle free. Once free, he wasted no time and climbed the castle wall, using his claws to create his hand holds in the stone. But Gargan didn't have to go very high before he felt the wind, and he leaped into the air, spreading his wings and letting the wind carry him up.

Bram, thinking he now had the upper hand, followed his nemesis. Gargan proceeded to put him on a wild chase through the skies. The two gargoyles put their gliding skills to the test as they raced in and around the castle towers and other fighting gargoyles. As Gargan completed another drastic turn, Bram anticipated it and slammed into the other gargoyle. Gargan started to fall out of the sky. Bram smiled as he watched the gargoyle fall but then three gargoyles flew past Bram and he lost his view of Gargan. Bram scanned the sky around and beneath him looking for any sign of Gargan. A few more moments went by and Bram started to think that perhaps he had won. Then from out of nowhere, a tremendous impact rocked him from above. Gargan had somehow snuck above him. Gargan slammed right on top of Bram, wrapping one arm around Bram's neck and the other through one of Bram's arms, locking it in place.

The initial impact knocked the wind out of Bram, and his wings, as he free-fell before righting himself. With Gargan locked on his back, he turned his whole body upside down as he glided, trying to unseat Gargan from his perch. But the gargoyle held firm. Bram tried a few other moves to free himself from Gargan's grasp, but nothing worked.

Gargan clenched his arm around Bram's neck even tighter. "It's over. Yield!" yelled Gargan with authority.

Bram responded by trying to use his free arm to reach and affect Gargan's hold, but with Gargan on top of him, Bram's free arm was no help.

"Yield," Gargan yelled again.

Bram tapped Gargan's arm, which was starting to suffocate him, in essence yielding to his enemy.

Gargan released the pressure, giving Bram just enough room. The evil gargoyle, seeing it as an opportunity, tried to twist and throw his free arm at Gargan's head. But Gargan knew Bram well. He knew the gargoyle would never truly yield and was prepared for Bram's desperate reaction. Gargan released his arm from Bram's neck as he dodged Bram's chaotic punch. They both started to fall from the sky as neither had time to be focused on gliding. But Gargan still had one of Bram's arms locked, and with this free arm, he sent a mighty punch towards Bram's head.

There was little Bram could do at close range and, turned around with his back to the ground, his wings were of little use. He tried to tear his one arm free from Gargan's grasp, but even as he did so, all he could do was watch the mighty fist coming toward him.

Gargan's punch hit him square in the face. Bram's face and head exploded in pain as the punch landed. The force of the blow sent Bram flying away from Gargan. Before Bram could even process the pain running through his head he went limp, the punch rendering him unconscious. Lifeless, Bram fell from the sky, and crashed at full force into the ground.

Gargan landed on the ground next to the unmoving Bram. Gargan's chest expanded and collapsed in quick succession, his breath coming fast. One more deep inhale and he started to recover.

He was slow and intentional as his gaze slid over to Bram, his long-time enemy. Mixed feelings came flooding over him.

Other gargoyles started to realize that Bram was knocked out of the sky and the fighting began to lessen. Gargan stood over his defeated enemy, wishing Bram would have yielded. He lay motionless on the ground. Gargan knelt on the ground, reached over, and probed the gargoyle's muscular neck, looking for a pulse. There was nothing. Bram's body was in rough shape, the long fall punishing it severely. A gargoyle's stone form can do wonderful things for an injured or even lifeless gargoyle. But there was no coming back from this. Bram was dead.

Gargan sighed. He stood back up and turned around. Just then he realized that the majority of the gargoyles, both his and Bram's clan, now stood around where Bram lay.

"Bram is dead," Gargan said in a somber tone, and not one that you would expect from a victor. "What does his clan now choose?"

A tall slender gargoyle stepped forward, raising his arm in the sky. "Our clan leader has been bested in combat. We will follow the ways of the gargoyles before us. Whoever beats a clan leader in combat earns the right to become the new clan leader."

Gargan nodded at the gargoyle. That was the result he was hoping for. But one gargoyle saying it didn't make it so. Gargan stepped away from the fallen Bram and addressed the whole group. "For years our two clans have been at odds. But now there is a new opportunity. We can end this fighting. We can end this rivalry between clans. Right now!" Gargan, paused, letting his words sink in. "In the way of the gargoyle I accept the leadership of your clan. But we are no longer two clans, we are one. We are now together, no longer enemies." Gargan looked around the group. Gargoyles from both sides seemed uneasy. None of them seemed to agree with his pronouncement. Gargan couldn't blame them; they had been enemies for years, and the last few years of direct combat would have created tremendous animosity.

"I know what you are thinking," said Gargan in a loud voice, re-capturing everyone's attention. "Why would I join these gargoyles standing next to me? And I will tell you why. There is now nothing to separate you. Bram is gone. Bram's schemes no longer exist. Those that followed Bram, speak now if you truly believe that the gate should be open. Speak now if you want to fight against all the other races. Speak now if you want the fighting to continue."

No one spoke.

Gargan nodded. "Those of my clan. What do you say? What reason is there to fight? The battle is won. Unite. Welcome these gargoyles, for they are now brethren."

Gargan stood and watched. Waited. Finally, the gargoyle known as Hawkins stepped forward and clasped hands with the tall slender gargoyle who had spoken from Bram's clan. That was all that was needed. All around gargoyles were clasping hands or shoulders. And Gargan was now the leader of one large, united clan.

Gargan let out a deep breath and took one step back toward his nemesis. Gargan had known this would be a possible outcome when he had suggested the idea to Lalatco and Leah. He had hoped somehow it wouldn't come to this. Looking back at the defeated Bram, Gargan shook his head. He had been the one to attack and force this final conflict. As much as it pained him to be the cause of this destruction, if it saved Jyres, and removed an enemy from the field, it was worth it.

9

Knives, Arrows, and Enemies at the Gate

Lalatco and Leah, with the help of the gargoyles, had reached the remnants of Stone Heights just before the sun came up. They had traveled the night and went without sleep. They were both happy with that, however, for it meant that the chances of having to fight gargoyles were almost non-existent. Just after the first rays of sunlight bathed the ruins, Lalatco and Leah made their way through the rocks. Remembering the last time they were here made it easy enough to find the entrance to the dungeon underneath the destroyed castle.

Despite feeling confident they would not run into any gargoyles, the two warriors still did not continue unprepared. Leah had an arrow knocked in her bowstring and Lalatco had two throwing knives in hand, his bandolier full of knives ready to supply him with more should he need them. Lalatco's heart beat in his chest with the anticipation of finding his friend. He was prepared for battle and no one would stop him from his mission of freeing Jyres. Leah processed similar emotions but in a different way. She took a deep breath and focused on the task at hand, as thinking of Jyres brought both smiles to her lips and tears to her eyes. She would not let her thoughts take her away from the present.

Lalatco led the way as they descended the steps into darkness. Squinting, but still trusting his vision, Lalatco and Leah made it to the bottom of the stairs without incident. Light was coming

55

through the entryway to the dungeon and Lalatco peaked around the corner. He saw two torches on the wall and eight orange and brown creatures spread out in the dungeon. Lalatco tucked his head back behind the wall and reported it to Leah in a hushed voice.

"Those creatures are chazz. I ran into a couple of them in my hunting days. They can be fierce up close because they have hard skin over their chests but they are a little slow. Aim for their necks or limbs, and move fast."

"Got it," said Lalatco, smiling at his wife while appreciating her knowledge. "I will take the left, you take the right."

Leah nodded. And as one they came around the corner into the dim light. Before the creatures even registered them as a threat Leah had let loose one arrow and was about to fire a second, while Lalatco had just thrown his second knife. Leah released her arrow and watched it strike its target in the neck, dropping it to the floor.

The husband and wife entered further into the room, and at last, the creatures responded. Four of them lay dead from the initial onslaught. As the creatures rushed toward the elf and human, an arrow dug into the leg of one of the chazz slowing its progress and a knife struck one in the eye, knocking it to the ground with screams of pain. Lalatco and Leah were proving to be too much for these creatures.

Lalatco pulled out his scimitar and Leah her sword as the two creatures who were still on their feet attacked. But their fate had already been decided. Lalatco sidestepped his attacker and slipped past, before slicing it behind its knees, sending it to the ground, where he ended its life before the creature had time to react.

Leah blocked a swipe of the second creature's arm and reversed her sword, slicing across the creature's opposite arm. The creature howled in pain before its cry was cut short by Leah's blade cutting its throat. Leah and Lalatco nodded at each other before focusing their attention on the two who had been slowed down but not killed. Leah and Lalatto dispatched the two creatures with ease.

It took a moment to realize that the commotion Jyres was hearing was real, and not just going on in his half-awake dream. As he came fully awake, he hurried over to the bars of his cell in time to see Leah cut down one of the orange and brown creatures. It was all but over before Jyres had even realized it was happening. A rush of emotion washed over Jyres as he watched his friends finish off the final two creatures. The happiness of his coming freedom was followed by tears of love. He knew all along that his friends would not abandon him. But in the long solitude he had experienced, it was hard to keep a level head. Now, seeing them here, he felt nothing but love and gratitude; it was overwhelming.

"My friends," Jyres half called and half gasped past the emotion. "I knew it was only a matter of time!"

Lalatco and Leah rushed over to his cell, each grabbing one of their friend's hands through the bars.

"Are you all right?" asked Leah as she reached her other hand through the bars, placing her hand on the side of Jyres's face.

He smiled at the gesture. "I am well, just hungry." He was about to ask them to get him out of the cell, but Lalatco was already ahead of him using one of his knives to force the lock open. As soon as the cell was open, Jyres stepped out and was greeted with hugs. The three embraced each other for a long while, no one speaking, just comforting each other with their actions.

Lalatco let go of the embrace and looked Jyres in the eyes. "I am so glad we have found you. Are you sure you are okay?"

Jyres smiled, "I am okay. And happy to be with you again my friend."

Leah finally stopped hugging Jyres and wiped a few tears from her eyes, tears of joy from seeing her friend unharmed.

Jyres let out a deep breath, thankful to be free. But fear and doubt also started to creep in on him as he realized that Elonda had not come with Lalatco and Leah. Jyres asked, "Where is Elonda? And Cyna? And the key, is it safe?"

There it was. Standing like an oasis in the surrounding emptiness. The Gate of Fire loomed large as the Silver Shadow and the horde stood just outside the ring of fire that encircled the gate. They were the only living beings anywhere to be seen. The local wildlife and creatures had decided to give this area a wide berth. Whether that was a conscious decision or one that had just happened over time was a guess.

The key was grasped so tight in his hand that it hurt. The Silver Shadow was unsure of how to proceed. On one hand, the Silver Shadow had accomplished much of what he had wanted to. On the other, more opportunity stood before him. His traveling to the area towns had done the trick. His name was once again spoken with fear and respect. It was a name people whispered about, afraid that saying it out loud would come back to haunt them in some unforeseen way. This gave the Silver Shadow much pleasure. And it left him wondering if this extra step was needed.

The Silver Shadow's gaze drifted from the key to the gate. Was it an opportunity, or death waiting for him? Would the horde see him as a partner or leader? Or was he merely a means to an end? But just think of the possibilities. If he was seen as more of a partner, or even a savior of their race, would he not control the most lethal army in the world? Would he not become the most powerful being known to man? Then his name would be feared like no other and the Silver Shadow would be known forever.

The horde stood next to him, not making a sound. Somehow patient, even though his brethren were stuck in that mystical world. The Silver Shadow knew his time was up. The horde had let him do what was needed in his personal quest, but now here they stood. The Silver Shadow, mind made up, stuffed the key in his pocket. Looking over at the horde, he nodded once, before stepping into the ring.

It was a weird feeling, an out-of-body experience at first. Even though the fire did provide some heat, he walked through untouched by the flames. The world took on a hazy glow as he took his first couple of steps into the ring and toward the gate. An old prophecy spoke of needing to conquer your fears in order to open the Gate of Fire. As the Silver Shadow took a few more determined steps he began to understand why. He saw the horde in front of him. Not just one creature, but a true horde. They stood before him as if he was talking to them, no, ordering them. All at once they rushed him, and he fell to the ground as they overwhelmed him.

The Silver Shadow's steps slowed, and he shook his head, trying to clear it of the disturbing images. Slower now he pressed on. Death? Who was he to fear death? Another step forward and his vision shifted. He stood, in grassland, no, in the middle of a town. And people walked by, oblivious to his presence, talking with one another. The Silver Shadow zeroed in on the conversations. "Did you hear about that Silver Shadow, what a joke!"

"I heard he lost all his power!"

"Power? What power?"

Conversations of this nature were all around him. And he came to a halt, his legs refusing to move.

He covered his ears with his hands and he fell to his knees. But the hands over his ears could not keep out the sound.

"Knight of Enchantment," laughed a woman, "More like a knight of lackluster."

"Who is this Silver Shadow?" asked another. "I have never heard of him."

"Exactly," and laughter ensued.

The Silver Shadow cried out, throwing his hands up. His greatest fear was being played out right in front of him. He couldn't make it stop. He couldn't move. He was trapped, overpowered by the fear assaulting him. The fear that he had been trying to make sure would never be a possibility. His name was on every tongue in every village. Yet here he was, a nobody.

The Silver Shadow could no longer differentiate between what was real and what was a creation of the ring of fire. His ability to rationalize, to think, was gone. There was only fire and fear. He lost all sense of time. He did not know how long he wallowed in fear, stuck in place inside the ring of fire. But all of a sudden, it was over and he was lying on the ground, just outside the ring.

The horde creature looked down on him. Assessing him.

Shaking his head to remove the last of the effects from the inferno that was the ring, the Silver Shadow rolled away from the horde, before standing and surveying the area around him. Everything appeared unchanged. He stood not far from where he had first entered the ring of fire. His gaze shifted toward the large Gate of Fire. He would never be able to pass through the fire and all the way to the gate. He knew that now. Knew that as much as he knew anything else. His fear was real. And it would not leave him.

The Silver Shadow realized the horde was staring at him. Waiting. The Silver Shadow threw his hands up. "I can't do it. It seems our partnership is over." The horde started to approach the knight. Once he had stepped close to him, he reached out his hand as if waiting for something to be given to him.

The Silver Shadow reacted by putting his hand into his pocket and clasping the key. But he paused. Is this what he wanted? Did he want the horde to have the key? Would the horde be able to pass through the fire? Or was that why the horde had been patient because he needed somebody? The Silver Shadow peered down at the waiting hand. *I am useless to this creature now*, he thought. I will not command his brethren, I will not hold a respected place among them. I am not their savior. I have failed. I will be cast out. Killed?

The Silver Shadow looked down at the offered hand one more time; and ran. He had no idea what he was going to do with the key from here. But he knew his fears would not allow him to open the gate. And he feared what the horde would do to him once they were all free. So he ran. Ran away from the horde, the gate, and the ring of fire, the ring where his fears had taken hold and driven him mad.

Although the dragons were unaware of it, Esmeralda and Crimson landed outside the ring of fire not long after the Silver Shadow had run off, the horde chasing him. The two dragons spread out along the front side of the ring of fire. There they stood, remaining vigilant as they guarded the gate.

10
Hope

The people at Serenity Castle displayed a mixture of excitement and trepidation. But a new seed had been planted. A seed of hope. Hope began when Vurth awoke from his long sleep. It grew when Lalatco, Leah, and Gargan arrived with a very-much-alive Jyres. And it blossomed with the news that Bram had been defeated.

The castle was alive with conversation, activity, and reunions. Word spread like wildfire throughout the castle upon the arrival of Jyres and his rescuers. People came running to see him and as soon as Jyres stepped through the gate he was being welcomed by the citizens of the castle. Vurth, for his part, was now up and about and he happened to be near the gate when his friends came walking through it. To say they were pleased to see him would be an understatement. As Jyres, Lalatco, Leah and Gargan gathered around him embracing him, it was hard to tell where one of them began and the other ended. Their arms and bodies became like one big knot.

Gargan agreed to go find the king and give him a report as Lalatco, Leah, and Jyres began asking Vurth how he was and any number of questions. Vurth shrugged them all away and focused their attention on Jyres. Jyres was overwhelmed by his welcome at the castle and was glad for it. But when he saw Cyna, he blocked out the others and swallowed her up in a fierce hug.

"Jyres, we were so worried," sobbed Cyna in between sniffles.

"I am here," Jyres replied.

A few moments went by before Cyna asked, "Did you see her yet?" A small smile made its way onto Cyna's face.

"Not yet," said Jyres, who didn't bother to try and hide his desire to see her. "But I am about to burst, where is she!"

"She is not far. I ran ahead as soon as we heard you were here." Cyna grabbed Jyres's hand and brother and sister started to walk through the throng of people. "She wasn't that far behind me," said Cyna as she tried to push through the crowd, leading Jyres.

Cyna said something else, but it was lost to the noise. Jyres had blocked it out, for he saw her. Elonda.

A small gap between the crowd started to form. At one side stood Jyres and on the other stood Elonda. Elonda's smile stretched from ear to ear and Jyres had never seen anything so beautiful in his life. His delight in seeing her showed all over his face. Elonda started to laugh before throwing her hands up to her face. Each hand cupped her cheeks. And then there were tears. Tears of joy.

Jyres did not wait any longer. He ran to her, closing the small space between them as fast as any human could. As soon as he reached her, Jyres threw his arms around Elonda, holding her close. She fell into his embrace. The whole gathered crowd fell silent, taking in the scene. Jyres and Elonda were both crying now, as they each let the joy they felt being back in each other's arms show. There they stood, an island of joy in a sea of quiet.

Jyres moved his hands from around her to her face. Elonda responded to his gentle urging and lifted her gaze to meet his. Jyres brushed away the tears with his thumbs, first from under the right eye, and then the left.

She smiled at him, a tentative smile. "Don't leave me again," she said.

"Never." Jyres pulled her face to his and kissed her.

The crowd erupted. Shouts, hoorays, laughs, claps and all manner of cheers radiated around the couple, bouncing off the stone walls as more cheers followed. Jyres and Elonda had forgotten about their audience and all they could do was laugh. After what had seemed like an eternity, the crowd started to disperse. Throughout all the fanfare, well-wishers, and the like, Jyres's and Elonda's hands were intertwined. Holding onto one another. Never letting go. As the final citizen moved on, Jyres, Elonda, Lalatco, Leah, Cyna, Vurth and Gargan, who had just returned, were left standing in a group. Each one bore a smile bigger than the person they were next to.

"Did they tell you about the dragons?" asked Cyna.

Jyres, confused, replied, "What about the dragons?"

"Come on, you have to see this!"

Jyres followed Cyna out of the castle, having to jog at times to keep up with the excited young girl. They went toward the back of the castle and the waterfall and then Jyres spotted them. Two young dragons. His mouth fell open, "But how? Where did they..."

Cyna laughed in response before saying, "Come on, I will introduce you." Cyna led Jyres by the hand and they crossed the valley to where the young dragons were relaxing. As they neared, Sunbeam sat up and Kaleido rolled over on the grass and shifted his neck to see who was approaching.

"Cyna," he exclaimed before getting up and bounding up to her.

"Hi there," Cyna replied as she patted his side. "This is Kaleido," she said while looking at Jyres before turning to point at Jyres. "This is my brother, Jyres."

"Very pleased to meet you," Jyres said with a nod.

The young dragon turned his neck to look back at Sunbeam. "I have a sister too. That is Sunbeam. She is a pain in my neck."

"Hey," Sunbeam roared before half-running into her brother. "Only because you are a pain in mine."

Jyres and Cyna laughed out loud, causing both dragons to look at them in confusion, which only caused the two humans to laugh even more.

"Unbelievable!" Jyres couldn't help but smile. He was unaware of the events that had brought two more dragons to this world, but he was happy for it. Two more dragons were never a bad thing, at least when they were on your side.

"Jyres," someone yelled.

Cyna and Jyres turned to see Tagro walking toward them. "It is time we catch you up on everything that has happened. The king is waiting to talk with you."

"Thanks, Tagro," Jyres shouted back. "I will be right there."

"Thank you," said Jyres looking over at his adopted sister. "Two more dragons…" Jyres's voice trailed off. "Escort me to the king?" Jyres offered Cyna his arm.

"Of course." Cyna slid her arm into Jyres's and walked with him back toward the castle. To their surprise, Elonda met them in the valley before they made it back to the castle. Elonda gave Jyres a quick hug before putting her hand in his left hand, his right arm still occupied by Cyna.

"Before you go to see the king, there is something you should know. Malick can fill you in on everything, but there is one item I thought that I would share with you." Elonda looked down at their hands, not sure how to continue.

"Okay. Go ahead. What's on your mind?" asked Jyres in a soft voice.

Cyna seemed to grab hold of Jyres's arm tighter as Elonda began speaking again. "I wanted to…well…" she blew out a breath and tried again. "I am sorry Jyres, but Zar is no longer with us. He has passed on."

The news hit Jyres like a battle axe. He closed his eyes and felt himself sink to the ground. His love and his sister stayed with him. Zar had been his mentor. In a lot of ways, he was the only mentor or father figure he ever had. In truth, they hadn't even known each other that long or spent an extensive amount of time together. But the time they had spent together was extraordinary. Zar had been there to walk Jyres through the prophecy, to help him, and to encourage him. Zar was there to protect him from his first interaction with the horde when it escaped the gate. Zar had saved his life when Jyres had been hurt by the horde. And now Zar was gone.

"How? When?"

In a gentle and quiet voice, Elonda responded. "Soon after you had been captured. He went peacefully. His time had come. Lumpkin told us."

"He was a great man. He will be missed," With a deep breath Jyres stood back up. He looked over at Elonda and Cyna. "Thank you for telling me and for being here with me."

They both hugged him and together they walked into the castle.

"Wow, that is a lot to take in," commented Jyres. The king had just finished filling him in on the events of the past days. Leah and Lalatco had told him some of this during their traveling back to Castle Serenity from Stone Heights. But they had agreed to let Elonda tell him about Zar and for the king to tell him the details of things like the ring of the seventeen, the antics of the Silver Shadow, and the belief that the yixl could be of help. "A lot has happened in so little time. Where do we stand in all this?"

"There is hope." King Malcik stood across from Jyres in the Throne Room. He turned as if looking at something and said, "The dragons have gone to protect the gate. They are there now. Some of the yixl are on their way to us." Malick paused, considering and turning back to Jyres. "We now know what the triangle is, and we have a way of communicating with the black donosin."

"Thank you for telling me all of this and thank you for sending my friends to rescue me. Judging by all that you have shared, I know you had a lot to manage." Jyres gave a slight bow, before starting to leave.

The king was quick to speak. "I have one more thing Jyres, if I may."

"Oh, yes, of course."

"Elonda made a comment to me while you were captured, and it is something that I would like to ask you about." Malick saw Jyres nod his approval, so he continued. "She was unhappy when I paired her with Mit to go to the yixl. And although she wouldn't go into details, it seemed to have something to do with how Mit had treated you."

Jyres gave a half smile, imagining Elonda's fiery reaction to the king's orders. "He used me in the deal with Heritage."

"Yes, you were key to solidifying our partnership with the city of Heritage." Malick was confused as this was not new information.

Jyres had tried to forget about this unfortunate experience, and for the most part, he had. He had moved on, thinking it was not helpful at this point to go back and revisit everything. But, he decided, the king had a right to know. "Well, there is a little more to it than that. The summary is, he led me and most of Heritage, to believe that my family was from that great city." Jyres paused, looking down for a moment and letting out a breath before continuing. "But in fact, there was no proof that my ancestors are from Heritage. It was what brought the citizens over to your cause; the lie tipped the scales and the treaty was signed." There, it was said. And hopefully, the last time he would have to think about it.

The king didn't respond at first, appearing to be in deep thought. After a few more moments went by the king lifted his head up. "I am truly sorry. I was not aware of the circumstances involved. I will think on this. I do appreciate you telling me this."

"Will that be all King Malick?"

"No, I don't think it will be." Malick stood and gave a short bow to Jyres. "I think I have been too hard on you Jyres, and have not given you the proper credit for how important you are to this kingdom." Malick walked forward to stand in front of the proclaimed Hero of Heritage. "Your arrival has sparked something in this castle, this battle, this...hope. I should have put more emphasis on finding you from the beginning." Malick reached out his hand.

Jyres returned the favor and the two shook hands. "Now, get some rest," the king said. "You will be needed; the fight goes on."

Jyres smiled, nodded, turned, and walked out of the Throne Room. He felt as though a bit of weight was off his shoulders, one less thing he had to carry around. His thoughts drifted back to what the king had said earlier. That there was hope. Hope was a funny thing. Jyres shook his head at the thought. Hope. What was hope? It was the desire for good things to come, the wish for certain things to happen. But where did hope come from, why was it there? It was there because you wanted to leave your current situation, you wanted to be in a better place. You hoped for a bright future. So yes, there was hope. But was hope blossoming because the alternative was despair? Their situation was anything but good and hope alone would not be enough. But a kingdom without hope was already lost. So despite their dire situation, Jyres chose to grab hold of hope and leave the despair behind.

The Silver Shadow had spent the last few days running and hiding. He was trying to stay ahead of, and undetected by, the horde. But other than that, he was at a loss for what to do next. If he wasn't in control of the horde and couldn't capitalize on the power and fear that would be created by letting them all on the loose on the world, then he wasn't sure he wanted them freed. So what is to be done with the key then? He could think of precious few options that made any sense. He couldn't think of anyone else who he would entrust with that kind of power. Maybe Meslar. But Meslar was no more. Meslar had made his attempt and the wizard had paid for it with his life.

So should he try and hide the key then, or did he just give it to the horde and leave the Kingdom of Calridian behind? There had to be some other life in this forsaken land. He had heard that there was some new race of creatures that the elves had found. Perhaps there were more out there somewhere. But even if he found said creatures, would they be far enough away from the horde? If he hid the key, what were the chances it stayed hidden? It had already been found twice before.

As the Silver Shadow processed these questions he stopped by a stream and knelt to refill his canteen with water. "Should I hide it?" He said out loud to no one. "Should I just let the horde have it?" The Silver Shadow shook his head, and sat down on the ground, watching the small stream flow around the rocks.

He pulled the key out of his pocket, tossed it in the air, caught it, and tossed it again. The key went up and down in a consistent rhythm. *Maybe I should throw it into this stream,* he thought. Be done with it and leave it for others to decide its fate. As he threw it up in the air and caught it one more time, a strong hand gripped his shoulder. Pain flooded his body, radiating from his shoulder and humming throughout his body. The Silver Shadow strained against the pain and turned his head to see what was happening. There, behind him, and holding on to him was the horde.

The Silver Shadow wanted to scream and wanted to tell him to stop. But he didn't have the strength. As he collapsed to the ground, his delga ability reacted and his form faded, before pulsing, his body's definition shifting in and out. The horde, unsure of what was happening, let go of his hold on the former knight.

The Silver Shadow let out a sigh of relief as the pain retreated. But something was not right. His ability continued to fade in and out. And he seemed to have no control over it. First, he was a shadow, then he was himself before it would again fade.

Then he was looking at himself. For just the briefest of moments, he was in two places. Both in bodily form and then as a shadow. His mind fought for where it should be — two entities asking for its ability to think, to process.

The horde grabbed onto the Silver Shadow once more. A scream erupted from the black-and-gray-clad knight. And as the body of the Silver Shadow breathed its last breath, the consciousness flew into the waiting shadow. The silver knight was no more.

All that remained was the Shadow.

The Shadow watched the creature take the key out of the hand of the dead body that used to be known as the Silver Shadow. The Shadow screamed but no sound came out. He rushed the horde, reaching for its arms as he did so. The horde did not react at all. It didn't even know the Shadow was there.

The Shadow's hands passed right through those of the horde. The Shadow looked down at his hands as the horde walked away. He tried to grab the horde's left hand with his right, and he couldn't do it. No! No! What has happened?

The Shadow's eyes then fell on the lifeless body in front of him. His greatest fears had been realized. The ring of fire had shown him his future. Here he lay lifeless. He was dead, yet he remained as this ghost. This shadow of himself. A shadow with no power. Not able to interact. A witness to his own death. Powerless. Powerless...

A scream of such agony and pain ripped from the Shadow. To the Shadow, it felt like the whole world had shaken. But to the world, not even a blade of grass shifted from the wind. Panic took hold of the Shadow. Sheer terror flooded him from all directions. The Shadow twisted left, and then right, and his whole form shook with violence. One more thought came to the Shadow as he sensed his ultimate end was near. Insignificance.

The Shadow convulsed. Convulsed again, and then burst. To the Shadow, his whole existence burst in an unbelievable display of smoke, wind, light, and energy. To the world, nothing discernable or of significance had happened.

Crimson and Esmeralda had been at the Gate of Fire for some time now. They often took turns keeping watch and resting, but neither found keeping watch all that interesting. As arc after arc slid by nothing happened. Nothing came even remotely close to the gate. So the dragons were bored and often both were doing more resting than watching. But even a dragon at rest can be an alert dragon.

Crimson lay on the ground, the hot sun was high in the sky and was roasting the poor dragon. He was resting on one side of the ring of fire, while Esmeralda lay on the other side. The large red dragon rolled over some, adjusting the scales and skin exposed to the most direct sunlight. The movement caused the dragon to open its eyes for a moment. And in that moment, Crimson saw a figure in the distance. The figure was small, but its direction was clear. It was walking towards the Gate of Fire. Unsure if it was the horde, or something else, Crimson called with a dragon roar to his partner Esmeralda.

Esmeralda landed near Crimson mere moments later. "What is it?"

"There," responded the male dragon. "Coming this direction."

As both dragons followed the progress of the figure in the distance, they fell silent, waiting to talk until there was something definitive.

"It is the horde," Esmeralda said sometime later. "I can see it now."

"But where is that knight he was with?" Crimson spat out the word "knight".

"It appears the horde is alone."

The two dragons stood like two pillars of strength and might as the horde came near. Esmeralda was unsure if they were strong enough to combat the powers of the horde. But she feared that they were going to have to find out, and very soon. Although she didn't know if the horde had the key, she couldn't think of another reason the horde would be approaching the gate. With that in mind, she turned to face her whole body toward the horde.

"That is far enough," roared Esmeralda at the approaching creature.

The horde stopped, as if in contemplation, then took another step. The dragons responded. Both of them shot a stream of fire right at the horde. For a moment the horde was engulfed in flame and couldn't be seen through the fire. But the fire seemed to circle around the creature before dissipating into the air. The horde took another step, with no evidence that the fire did anything at all to it.

The two dragons shared a look of concern as the fire finished its disappearing act. Then the horde continued its progress. After the horde took a few more steps Crimson reacted by swinging his long tail at the creature. The creature paused as the tail seemed to go right through the gelatinous form that was the horde. After the small pause, the horde took another step. Esmeralda spotted the key in the horde's hand and tried to slash the creature with her razor-sharp claws. But those, too, seemed to do little against the enemy. Crimson moved to block the way to the gate, putting his large frame in the path of the horde. The horde reached out, touching the dragon with both hands. As soon as the horde contacted the mighty dragon, the dragon recoiled from the contact. Crimson had felt instant pain.

The dragons knew they were running out of options. Nothing they tried seemed to make any difference. The horde just kept on moving toward the gate. The Gate of Fire stood waiting. The horde's brethren were waiting. Panic flashed in Esmeralda's eyes as she envisioned the land covered by the horde creatures. With no other options, Esmeralda maneuvered behind the horde. She opened her maw wide and extended her neck. Then she closed her mouth around the horde. As soon as she had done so, her whole mouth, and then her head, felt like they were being stabbed from the inside. For the briefest of moments, Esmeralda thought about swallowing the horde. But too afraid of what the result would be, she spat the creature out, sending it spiraling away from the ring of fire. But even then, the damage had been done, and Esmeralda slumped to the ground, still in pain from the prolonged contact.

Crimson, seeing his partner gasping for breath on the ground, charged the horde. The horde was just getting itself up off the ground after being spat out when a charging dragon ran right through it. The horde's body seemed to stretch and bend as the behemoth passed through it. It did slow the horde for a moment or two, but then, as if this was just prolonging the inevitable, the horde began walking toward the Gate of Fire again.

Esmeralda had not yet recovered her strength, and Crimson was at a loss for what to try next. This left the two dragons with no options, the mighty creatures brought low. They watched in pure agony and fright, as the horde, with the key in hand, walked up to the ring of fire. If the creature took one more step it would be in the ring and on its way to the gate and its brethren. And the world would be lost...

Crimson, in a fit of rage and panic, charged at the creature. As he charged, a last-ditch idea came to him. Just before the horde stepped into the ring, Crimson clamped two of its big fangs right onto the key in the horde's hand. Crimson didn't waste any time and immediately took flight. Crimson pumped his wings, gaining height and then racing to the north. The key was in its jaws, and the horde was holding onto it and hanging from the dragon as it flew. Crimson beat his wings, putting as much space between the gate and the horde as possible. He tossed his head in erratic patterns, trying to lose the horde, still holding on to the key.

The horde would not let go. After all this time, it had been so close. It grabbed onto one of the dragon's large teeth with one hand, holding onto the key with the other. As it got whipped from one side to the other the horde held firm. Crimson started to feel pain radiating from his mouth as he began to feel the touch of the horde. Still, he soared on to the north. But then the horde swung his legs onto the dragon's mouth, and his whole mouth started to feel the pain. Still, Crimson would not let go of his hold on the key.

He tried again, in chaotic fashion to loosen the horde's hold on the key. But the key seemed to be a part of that gelatinous hand and he could not dislodge the horde. It came to a point when the mighty dragon could bear the pain no longer, he swung his massive head one more time, this time letting go of the key.

The horde and the key went spiraling away into the sky. Crimson watched the horde in its free-fall, well to the north of the old city of Secord. The dragon had no idea if the horde would survive the fall from such a height, but he had no reason to think that it wouldn't. Crimson was tiring fast, the horde's prolonged touch doing its damage. Crimson completed a slow turn, heading back the way he had come. Little by little, he drew closer to his partner. Both of them were battered and weakened. But by an instinctive action, Crimson had saved them for now, bought them some more time. It would take many days for the horde to travel on foot back to the gate. And for that Crimson was thankful because as he landed by Esmeralda, it seemed that they would both need much time to recover.

12
Wondering by the Wanderer

The man of nature, formerly known as Bartholomew the Bold, stood on a small hill feeling the strong breeze as it blew around him. He now went by the name of the Wanderer. Without thinking, he dropped his hand to his necklace made of bones. He tapped his fingers along the individual pieces as he pondered things over in his mind. He felt something, he could feel it in the air and in the very soul of the world around him. Kneeling, he dug his hands into the dirt and held them there.

The Wanderer, a delga whose abilities made him one with the land and animals, was leaning into those abilities now. He relaxed, closed his eyes, and waited. Feelings started to come to him, he felt the emotions of the nearby animals, the mood of the land, and the health of the trees. The breeze brought with it the smells of dirt, trees, and creatures. All this he took in, but what he was searching for alluded him. Something was there, waiting for him to find it.

The Wanderer sighed and stood up as slow raindrops started to fall. He had been bothered by this feeling for a few arcs now. But he had been unable to identify the place from where this sensation was emanating. He had pondered returning to see the black donosin, a race with whom he shared a special bond. He wondered whether, in their presence, more answers would come to him. But in the end, he had decided to travel in the direction of Alhazar. It hadn't been that long since he was last there, but if the land was telling him something was about to happen or was already happening, it seemed to be the most likely place to investigate.

The Wanderer heard just a hint of something stirring, and then he smelled someone near. His hands flew to his back where his two-handed, double-edged sword was sheathed. He had it out with lightning speed as he pivoted on his left leg to turn toward whoever it was that had snuck up on him.

Not more than three sword lengths away stood the large and imposing figure of Demorous. The bald delga was smiling and he offered a wave to the man of nature. "I didn't think I would be able to get this close to you. Perhaps my skills are improving."

"Or perhaps I allowed myself to be distracted, that would seem to be more plausible," responded the Wanderer with a chuckle.

"A few people have been looking for you."

"Looking for me?" asked the Wanderer. "Why? I can't be that hard to find!"

"I don't know much, but something about a Bear's Heart." The big delga stroked his long dark beard. "Apparently, they think you can help them with it."

The Wanderer said nothing at first. He took a moment to sheath his sword and crossed his arms before he began pacing. The rain fell a little harder now, and Demorous wiped the water from his face as he stood and watched the Wanderer, letting him do whatever it was that he needed to do. But after a while he got impatient.

"So, are you just going to walk back and forth all day, because believe it or not, it gets kind of boring to watch." Demorous gave the other delga a smile at the end of the statement, but what he said was pretty much how he felt. He was Demorous the Fierce. Not Demorous the Patient. And since it was raining, patience was nowhere in sight.

"I need to return to the donosin. I am unsure..." the Wanderer's voice trailed off.

"Hey, I am supposed to bring you back to the castle. The Envoy could not find you, so I am here. Why don't you come back with me to the castle and you can do more thinking there, or talk to the waterfall or whatever."

The Wanderer looked back at his former fellow knight, at first with a glare, but he was quick to soften it. The Wanderer knew people didn't understand his powers, and that was fine. He just needed to remind himself of that every once in a while. "You know that is not quite how it works," he said with a smirk. "Besides, something else has also been gnawing at me. I need to be back with the black donosin." With this new mystery about a Bear's Heart, it now pointed at a return to the donosin instead of Alhazar.

"Come on Bartholomew," Demorous said, slipping into his old ways. "Sorry, Wanderer."

"Listen, I assume they are asking me about the Bear's Heart because I have contact with the greatest of bears. Correct?"

"I would assume," the big delga replied, waving his arm to urge his friend to continue talking.

"Well, right at the moment, I do not think I can be of assistance. So I need to return to the donosin's enclave. Hopefully, I can learn more there." A pause, and then, "Besides, it appears as though that is where nature is telling me to go."

"Well, what am I supposed to tell King Malick then? He is expecting me to walk in with you by my side." Demorous finished by gesturing to a spot next to him.

"Tell him you found me. Tell him what I am telling you."

Demorous rolled his eyes. He hadn't always understood his fellow delga, and this was a case in point right here. It didn't make much sense to him, but he could remember a reason why he wouldn't want to trust the Wanderer. However, after Meslar messed with all of their minds, the details sometimes got a little murky. But he did recall taking a liking to Bartholomew. "Well, get on with it then," he said after the extended silence.

"I will tell you what." The Wanderer bent down, placing one knee on the ground. "I can do just a little better than that." The Wanderer put his hand flat on the ground, closed his eyes, and took a deep breath. After a moment a small fox emerged from the field and approached the Wanderer at a slow pace.

Demorous watched as the Wanderer reached out and put a hand on the bright red fox. The fox flinched at first but then stood still as the Wanderer began petting the fox and whispering some sort of nonsense that Demorous could not make out. The fox looked over at him, before trotting up and sitting right down next to him.

"Oh, you have got to be kidding me! What is this Bartholomew? If this is some silly prank..." Demorous's hands were in the air emphasizing his unhappiness with the situation.

The Wanderer couldn't help but laugh, watching the small fox sit unassuming next to the large specimen that was Demorous the Fierce. "No, no, no intentional prank. Though now that I think about it, the small fox may not add to the fierceness of Demorous."

"Oh...for.." Demorous covered his face with the palm of his hand.

"No, the fox has another purpose. When the time is right, you or whoever the king deems fit, can follow the fox and she will lead you to my location."

"Okay, um, how am I going to know if the time is right?"

"The fox will tell you." The Wanderer started to turn but stopped, and said, "The fox is a she, by the way, and her name is Mezza."

"It has a name?" yelled Demorous.

The Wanderer started to walk away, giving a wave to his back as he did so.

"Ahhh," groaned Demorous. "Seriously, what am I supposed to do with this thing until it is the right time." Demorous putting up air quotes with his fingers on the last phrase.

"Feed it!" yelled the Wanderer.

Demorous just shook his head. He looked up as the rain continued to come down and then, looking toward the fox, he said, "So, now what?"

The fox just wagged its tail once as it stood staring at Demorous.

"Well, come on then." Demorous started to walk back towards where he had left his horse a short distance away. Mezza followed right along and stopped when they had reached the horse. As the former knight began mounting his horse, the fox jumped on a nearby fallen tree and used that new height to leap up onto the back of the horse, landing right behind the saddle. The well-trained horse reacted with a slight step to the right but maintained his position enough for his rider to finish swinging his leg over the saddle. Demorous was beside himself. "What do you think you are doing!" he yelled at the fox. "You can walk."

The fox didn't move.

Demorous swatted a hand in the fox's direction, but that did nothing to deter the red fox either. "Oh, for... have it your way." As the horse started off at a comfortable trot, Demorous shook his head. "That dwarf can't hear a thing about this, or I will never hear the end of it."

13

Click-Clack

Rutu and six of his friends who volunteered to help him had made the long journey to Alhazar. They could see the Valley of the Dragons now to the north and east. But Rutu had decided that they would camp for the night and finish the journey in the morning. They had gone a long way on this day, and Rutu wanted to arrive refreshed. The group of seven yixl huddled around a small fire, clicking and clacking to each other in their unique language. As Rutu looked around at his friends, the fire seemed to dance in their large dark eyes. Rutu joined the conversation as one of the yixl was telling stories, causing much laughter in the group. But Rutu was quick to cut them off and put a finger to his lips. The yixl each let their hand fall to the long knife at their side as they made slow deliberate moves and turned away from the fire.

Out of the shadows melted ten goblins. The goblins came forward and the yixl noticed that they were equal in size to themselves, and held similar weapons. The yixl made a complete, tight circle around the fire as the goblins encircled them.

"Whos is this?" asked one goblin.

"I don't knows," replied the skinny goblin who had strips of blue cloth tied around each bicep. "A new smell I smell."

"As long as they tasty." A third goblin laughed.

This goblin group was a collection of outcasts and outside the influence of the orc, and self-appointed leader, Ogla. The goblin marked with blue was the leader of the small band and he had been banished from the mountain homes. He was simply known as Bluey and had picked up his followers over the last several days. And they believed they had come across an easy target, seeing that they had the numbers over the unknown species. With a large smile on his scarred face, Bluey yelled a battle cry and the goblins rushed at the yixl.

But they knew nothing about Rutu and this group of yixl. As the goblins rushed in, Rutu yelled his instructions. Each yixl stabbed a log in the fire with their long knives, accepting the short-term heat from the fire. Almost in perfect unison, the yixl turned back toward the goblins just before they struck, with a burning log waiting for them. Goblins shrieked as a few received burns to their arms or face. Rutu click-clacked again and the yixl raised their knives and brought them forward in a rapid motion, sending the burning logs at the surprised goblins. More goblins screamed as they were hit by flying logs. As the goblins tried to recover, the yixl attacked. Four of the goblins received knife wounds and fell to the ground in panic and pain.

Bluey, seeing that his targets were no easy catch, turned and ran, and the rest of the goblins were quick to follow.

As the goblins retreated with their shrieks they heard the yixl ushering them away. "Click. Clack. Click. Clack," they all yelled in unison, raising their knives on the clack. Their chatting slowly turned into laughing and the yixl patted each other on their scaley heads. They then retrieved the logs and returned them to the fire, having to stomp out a few sparks of fire on the grass around them. As they gathered around the fire once again, the yixl were all smiles. It was rare that the yixl were in combat, but Rutu and this select group of friends had trained together well. The current yixl leader was against anything that involved violence or the possibility of yixl being hurt. A few conflicts had arisen with the Shepherds of the Isles over the years, but even those had been limited whenever possible. So this small band of yixl enjoyed the chance to beat those goblins away.

Bluey cursed and yelled as he ran. The click-clacks would see Bluey again. Bluey hates to lose. Bluey held grudges. "Click-clack!!" he screamed so hard that spit flew everywhere.

Ogla had somehow done something that few had ever been able to do. Over the last few years, Ogla the orc had been able to bring some semblance of authority and organization to the numerous groups of orcs and goblins that lived in the mountains of Alhazar. In fact, no major orc or goblin raid had been made outside of the mountains since Meslar had worked his magic those few years ago. That in itself was an amazing feat but Ogla had also brought some organization to the many tunnels under the mountains. Now, though chaos still reigned there, it was said that venturing in to the tunnels no longer meant an automatic death as in years past, though that was still a strong possibility. Infighting had lessened as well. But even with all of that impressive progress, there were still orcs and goblins that would always be a problem.

One such goblin went by the name Bluey. He had become known as Bluey because of the strips of blue cloth he had tied around each bicep. Bluey had caused one fight after another in the goblin tunnels, which, in time, led to Ogla kicking him out, and almost killing him in the process. Bluey was left with a long scar across his forehead and another across one of his pale green legs.

Just thinking of the name Ogla often sent Bluey off on a rampage of the mouth, and he took it out on anyone who happened to be near him. But Bluey was a survivor. He had lost count of the near-death experiences he had faced. To be fair, the rate of these occurrences for goblins was much higher than that of the other races. But...by all rights and percentages, Bluey should be dead. But he wasn't. And he had no plans of dying anytime soon. It was this trait that drew other riffraff to him. It wasn't because of his amazing battle prowess or his ability to lead. The scum were drawn to him because he was somehow still alive. And they figured if some of that skill, or maybe it was luck, rubbed off on them, then they would stay alive as well. That luck didn't work for one goblin during the last battle. He died from his wounds.

Bluey led the remainder of his group of goblins back to their temporary campsite where they could lick their wounds. They had set up to the west of the river Mitelow on one of the small tributaries. They found a spot where the ground had eroded near the river bank, leaving an overhang that provided a little bit of cover. Once there, it didn't take long for the goblins to start complaining to Bluey.

"They were nots easy," complained one goblin in a sniveling voice.

Bluey did not hold back. He was as frustrated as any of them. "You did nothings!" he shouted at them as he sat down on a log. Bluey pulled out his knife and stabbed it into the sand.

"Not easy ats all."

"Nothings!" Bluey called again, ignoring any more of their complaints. He had two on his list now. Ogla and the click-clacks. And once someone was on Bluey's list they either died, or Bluey got more scars. He didn't have a big enough crew to go after Ogla. Not yet. But the click-clacks, he wasn't convinced that his crew couldn't beat them. This would not be the last they saw of him. They would track them in the morning and learn more about the click-clacks.

14

An Alchemist at Work

King Malick had sent a number of his envoys to find the Wanderer and ask him questions about the black donosin and the Bear's Heart. But they had struggled to find him. Malick was, then, quite surprised when Demorous showed up at the castle with news of the Wanderer. News and also a fox who would never seem to leave the former knight's side. Malick remained frustrated about the situation, however, considering that they had to wait for the fox to somehow tell them it was time to come find the Wanderer. Demorous's story seemed far-fetched, but there was no reason for Demorous not to tell the truth, and the fox seemed to be pretty good proof of the former knight's claims.

In anticipation of finding the Wanderer, the king had called together the Council, knowing that even if the Wanderer was not found, decisions would still need to be made. This was the first time the entire Council was able to be in attendance since the Day of Two Moons. The Council had gathered in the great hall and met at night, as was their custom, since Gargan was in his stone form during the day. Much was discussed, as much had happened, and not all on the Council were aware of the complete picture. To summarize the meeting, the king stood and looked in turn at each of the gathered members.

"Here is where we stand. The horde has the key but is many days north of the gate. Crimson and Esmeralda," the king nodded his thanks to the emerald dragon, "were able to fend off the horde for now, though it came at a price. And we cannot depend on that tactic again." The king paused as others gave the dragon their thanks. "We now know what the triangle is and we are waiting for word from the Wanderer, hoping he can learn about the Bear's Heart. We just received a report that the yixl will be here in the morning and had to fight off a group of goblins during the night. Now is the time for decisions." Malick sat back down, giving everyone a moment.

"How are we hoping that the yixl will help us?" asked Carrie, voicing the question that others were most likely thinking.

"I assume," said Lord Kapel, "given their ability to withstand the horde, that we plan on sending the yixl to the gate to defend it. Much like the dragons did."

"How many yixl are coming?" asked Empress Octavia.

The king nodded, knowing the question would be asked. "Our scout tells us seven."

"May I suggest another plan," said the rough voice of Shepherd Roland, the Warden of Skystair. "I was talking with that interesting dwarf...what was his...oh yes, Lumpkin. I was talking with Lumpkin, and with a sample of the yixl's spikes, he may be able to craft a potion to help us."

"How exactly would a potion help us in this situation?" a couple of council members asked at the same time.

"Well, I was a little unclear on that part; he's a hard dwarf to comprehend sometimes."

The others laughed, despite the circumstances, while recalling the dwarf's uniqueness.

"Even if we assume we can find the Bear's Heart, and use the yixl, there is still one more thing that needs to be addressed." Lord Kapel was talking again. "I think it is time you let us in on your plan for the delga wizard. For we will require one of those as well."

King Malick nodded. "Yes. The young girl, Cyna, is a delga and has shown the abilities of a wizard, though those abilities are still undeveloped."

This caught many members by surprise, and a few gasps were heard around the room. The girl's true nature had been kept hidden from many, including those on the Council. Gargan spoke first. "Jyres will not like whatever it is you have planned for his sister."

Others started to talk all at once and the room turned into loud bickering.

"Quiet," thundered Esmeralda. "It is the only option." Not many things can calm a crowd down like the voice of a dragon.

"So, we plan to assemble the Ring of the Seventeen," stated the king. "The Bear's Heart. The delga wizard, Cyna. Three of each of the triangle. Three dragons. Esmeralda can decide how the dragons will be positioned. Three black donosin. We will assume that the Wanderer will provide them for us. Three delga. We have a few options, Lord Kapel will decide. And six other races. We have humans, elves, dwarfs, yixl, gargoyles, and an orc." The king looked over the group as they processed everything that he was saying.

Vurth grunted but didn't say anything as others looked on. Vurth had never grown all that comfortable with Ogla. He had heard too many stories and had too many bad experiences with orcs to ever put his complete trust in one. But here they were, asking one of them to take a place in the Ring of the Seventeen. But Ogla was on the Council and had shown no reason not to trust him. So who was he to speak out against the orc?

Soon after the planning of the Ring of the Seventeen was complete, the king dismissed the Council with promises of more information to come.

Rutu and his yixl companions arrived to little fanfare. Although the Council was more than happy that they had arrived, the castle's citizens seemed to take little notice. But that was all well and good for the king was able to see Rutu right away. As luck would have it, Karth and Brigand had also arrived. Although they had left after the yixl, they rode on horses and made up time, allowing them to arrive in a timely fashion. Malick had to rely on Karth for translation and was appreciative of it. After a long conversation, Rutu and Karth left their audience with the king and sought out Lumpkin as instructed.

Karth had a difficult time translating for the odd dwarf and the outgoing yixl. But by the end of the conversation they had arrived where they needed to be. Rutu sat still for Lumpkin as Karth had instructed. The dwarf moved with precision as he scraped one of the yixl's spikes with his tool. Any residue that Lumpkin was able to collect, he transferred from his tool to a jar. He did this a couple of times before motioning to Rutu and Karth that he was finished.

A look of surprise, and maybe relief, flashed across Rutu's lizard-like face. Perhaps the translation hadn't been perfect Karth realized. But it was better that Lumpkin needed less from Rutu than he expected than the other way around. Karth led Rutu out of the room, leaving Lumpkin to work.

The dwarven alchemist started by studying and evaluating the spike fragments he had collected. He took one little speck of the spike and put it in a separate container. Once there he reached into his jacket, the vials bumping each other as he did so, creating the tinkling and clicks that most people just associated with the peculiar dwarf. Finding the one he wanted, Lumpkin pulled out the stopper and let one drip of the pink liquid fall into the container he had set aside. Lumpkin watched for the reaction that the potion had with the speck. Lumpkin gave a slight frown, as no reaction seemed to take place at all.

Lumpkin had developed a few potions over the years that helped break down rock and other materials. He also had a couple of potions that he had tried in the past to duplicate items. These had come with mixed results. With these potions, bits of yixl spikes, and his alchemist knowledge, he hoped to supply something in the form of a weapon or spell that would be able to combat the horde.

Lumpkin worked nonstop for the whole morning before breaking for a quick lunch. After lunch, he felt he was maybe starting to get somewhere when there was a knock at the door. Lumpkin paused what he was doing and went to open the door. There stood Cyna. The smiling young girl seemed happy to see him.

"Hi, Lumpkin, how is your work going?" Cyna asked as she stepped into the small room and started inspecting everything he had laid out on what had become his work table.

"Okay, okay, maybe progress," replied the dwarf as he used a small metal tool to squeeze one small piece of the yixl spike and bring it closer to his face for examination. Putting it back down on the table, he crossed his arms and let out a "humph." Lumpkin reached for another potion in his coat of many pockets and let some of the brown liquid drop onto the metal tool that was still squeezing a sliver of the spike. This time it created a reaction, a quick puff of smoke was released as the liquid contacted the sliver.

Cyna, who had been watching the dwarf the whole time, noticed his excitement at whatever the brown liquid did. She continued watching as he scraped all of his spike fragments together and dropped more brown liquid on it, creating a bigger puff of smoke. Cyna had no idea what the dwarf was doing but enjoyed watching him work as his excitement built. The dwarf grabbed a different vial from his coat this time. It was green in color but had a tint of pink as well. Lumpkin seemed to take his time with this one and was slow to pull the stopper out of the vial and then was more than careful as he let two drops from the potion land on the fragments. Cyna watched in amazement as the fragments bubbled and then bounced, and an identical number of pieces of yixl spike landed right next to the original.

Lumpkin let out a whoop, "See? Did you see? I did it! Did it!" exclaimed the dwarf.

Cyna raised her arms in a cheer. "Good job, Lumpkin!"

But Lumpkin raised his finger; he had one more thing to do. He picked the brown potion up again. This time he poured a drop or two on the newly copied fragments. Lumpkin and Cyna both watched in anticipation. Cyna had watched enough now to know that the dwarf hoped for a puff of smoke to come from the new spike materials. But as they both looked on, no puff of smoke was created.

Lumpkin sat back on his stool, his face a gnarl of confusion. He had been able to duplicate the objects, but they failed to retain the original properties.

"Something I can help with?" asked the always curious Cyna. As she waited for his response, she picked up the staff from the corner of the room. The staff had a purple delga stone set into the top of the wood. The staff once belonged to Meslar, but Zar had passed it to Lumpkin now. The staff had been shortened by a considerable amount to accommodate the height of the dwarf. Cyna held it in one outstretched hand and rotated it as she examined it.

At first, Lumpkin just shook his head. He turned to watch Cyna as she moved the staff, and that gave him an idea. He reacted so fast that he almost fell off his stool. "Come, here, come!" he shouted to the young girl.

This caught Cyna by surprise but she did what she was asked, bringing the staff with her. "Lumpkin, what is it?" she asked as she approached the table.

"You spell. Do a spell...," he stammered as he prepared the table, quickly re-stopping vials and putting things back in their place.

Cyna still didn't quite understand what he was asking. She watched him in nervous anticipation as he finished cleaning the table, leaving just the original spike fragments in the middle of the table. "Lumpkin, I can't even lift rocks anymore, what is it you think I can do?"

Lumpkin pointed at the delga stone sitting on top of the staff. "Hands. In your hands, stone...stone will help. Here, this first," said Lumpkin as he placed a rock on the floor. "First."

Cyna looked at the dwarf, exhaled, and turned her gaze to the rock sitting on the floor. She had tried to move rocks and hadn't been successful since that fateful night. Why would this make a difference? She shifted her stance toward the rock, taking another breath. Then pointing the staff at the rock she yelled, "Stovea!" She felt the power of the delga stone coursing through her and her eyes went wide as the rock started to lift off the ground. The stone on the staff glowed a deep bright purple.

"See," exclaimed Lumpkin. "You can! You can!"

Cyna couldn't help but smile as she watched the rock float all the way to the ceiling. She lowered the staff, felt the power lessen, and watched as the rock succumbed to gravity and fell back to the floor, landing with a clatter. After a moment the adrenaline wore off and Cyna felt a wave of tiredness, but it was gone as soon as it came.

Lumpkin ran to her jumping up and down. "Together, we do it! Do it together."

Cyna shook her head in acknowledgment, "What do you need me to do?"

Lumpkin led her over to the table and urged her to sit down as he pulled out an old book. He had found this one at the library and had kept it with him, as it was full of spells and potions, and it came in handy. He turned the pages in the leather-bound book until he came to the page he was looking for. It had a depiction of duplication drawn out and words above and below the drawing. The words were in an old language, an ancient language filled with words of power.

"I have done work. The work is done." Lumpkin pointed at the illustrations while holding up his potion. "But I need delga power. Need your power, complete it well." Lumpkin pointed to the words at the bottom.

Cyna looked them over, trying to work out in her head how they would be pronounced. "But I don't know how to say the words." Cyna's heart was racing. She was worried. All of a sudden, everything felt too real. Her breathing came fast. She gripped the table with both hands and stared down at the floor, gasping for breath. A callused hand slid over the top of her left hand, and she grasped it. Her breathing slowed, and the young girl raised her head again. "Thank you."

"Yes, Yes. I know words, most words. Listen." Lumpkin grabbed both of Cyna's hands in his, leaving the staff to rest against the table. "Don't think about. Look at me. Me."

Once he had her attention and was convinced he was the focus and she wouldn't accidentally start an actual spell, they began. Together they practiced the words that went with the duplication spell. Lumpkin didn't always know every word in the old language, but for the most part he had been able to get a solid understanding of the inflections and pronunciations needed for the ancient words.

After a lot of repetitions, Lumpkin nodded. "You are ready."

15

The Fox and the Found

D emorous walked out of the castle, a new day had just begun. The pleasant sunshine and warm fall day were a sharp contrast to the feelings and mood of some of the citizens of the Kingdom of Calridian. For his part, he didn't get as wrapped up in all the what-ifs. It was a new day and so far they were all still here. The red fox, his constant companion came running after him. "Mezza, thought maybe I got away from you there," said the big man. The two of them kept walking in the sun before Demorous did a quick turnaround to go back to the castle.

"Demorous," cried Vurth in laughter. "What is that you got there, a pet?" The dwarf had spotted Demorous and started walking towards him.

Demorous let out a sigh and closed his eyes. He hadn't turned around fast enough. Well, nothing to do about it now. "Vurth, you are not dead!"

"Why, no, not yet. Still some life left in this stubborn dwarf. But don't change the subject. What is this furry little thing that is now following around Demorous the Fierce? I had heard about it but needed to see it for myself." The dwarf started laughing, slapping his knee as he did so.

"Keep laughing dwarf. We will see who is laughing when this little fella saves the day!"

That just made Vurth laugh even harder. Vurth slapped the big delga across the back, "Well, that would be something!"

Demorous just shook his head at the dwarf's antics. He knew all along that Vurth would enjoy this just a little too much. Demorous was sure that the Wanderer had done this on purpose. He probably had many ways that he could have achieved what he wanted. But he just had to have a little fox follow Demorous the Fierce around. Demorous looked down at the fox, sitting nice and quiet beside him, waiting for whatever Demorous was going to do next.

But then something changed. Mezza's ears perked up as if it was straining to hear something. Then she stood up, focused on whatever she was hearing or sensing. After a moment she tilted her head up to Demorous and looked him in the eyes. Then she started to walk toward the entrance to the valley. But she didn't go very far before looking back at the big delga.

Demorous was unsure of what had just happened and he noticed Vurth was also watching the fox. At first, Demorous didn't do anything, just stood watching Mezza, who just stood there looking back at him. Shrugging, Demorous took a couple of steps forward and Mezza started moving again. Demorous stopped, and so did the fox.

"Well, it appears it wants you to follow it," said Vurth. His tone showed his attitude had changed from humor to curiosity.

"I think you are right. Perhaps the Wanderer has need of us." Demorous paused as he thought through the situation. "I think I will go ready a horse, who knows where the fox will lead me."

"Aye, good idea. Saddle two horses. I will go fetch some supplies."

Demorous couldn't keep the surprise from his face. "Two horses?"

"I must admit, the little rascal has me curious," chuckled the dwarf.

The fox waited, as quiet as a mouse, as Vurth and Demorous readied the horses and supplies and reported to the king. Once they were each astride a horse and trotting toward Mezza, only then did the fox start walking again.

"Where do you suppose it will lead us?" asked Demorous.

"I have no idea, maybe it just has a favorite spot to relieve itself," laughed the dwarf in reply.

Even Demorous had to laugh at that thought. With two laughing riders the horses followed the fox out of the valley. They were both quite surprised later on when they realized the fox was leading them to the mountain pass.

The mountain pass was created long ago when the dragons led others to this side of the mountains in a quest for peace. Although that peace had lasted a long time, and the two sides of the mountains had now been united as one kingdom, it all seemed to be in danger now. The horde had proven it had the capability to not only disrupt peace but also to destroy the kingdom, one interaction at a time. And somehow, this small fox was now playing a role in the kingdom's reaction to the horde. It reminded Demorous of Jyres in a way. When Meslar had started his quest for the gate, Jyres, a human, who was thought of as a lesser being at the time, found himself at the heart of the conflict.

Demorous shook his head at the memory. Demorous showed his fierce side to Jyres on more than one occasion. But at the time he had been under Meslar's magical influence. Still, it bothered Demorous. He knew Jyres had forgiven the knights, in fact, it was Jyres who first said that the knights were no longer enemies. But Demorous hoped he would find a way to make it up to him, whether Jyres thought it was needed or not.

The fox continued to lead the way as darkness fell and the night moon was visible in the sky. The horses had just started following the mountain pass, something that in the past would have been a dangerous endeavor. But the king had issued orders for outposts to be built along the main passageways, and under Vurth's watchful eye, one had been built along the mountain pass. The outpost in the mountains was the largest one built, allowing a bigger group of soldiers to be stationed there.

Vurth saw this trip as a good opportunity to check on his charges and ensure they were doing their job well. If they were, the paths would be kept safe from the goblins and orcs who were always near the area. Ogla's reach only extended so far, and lone travelers would have been easy targets had it not been for the outpost and its guards. An arc or so later, Vurth spotted a group of three dwarves huddled near the path. Vurth could have announced himself as soon as he noticed them but decided to let it play out so he could observe the dwarves as they worked. A moment or two later, one of the dwarves called out to the two travelers.

"Hello," came the rough voice, "Who travels the mountain pass?"

Demorous was about to respond but Vurth signalled him to remain quiet. Their horses walked on, neither rider answered the call.

This time three dwarves stepped out into the middle of the path as one lit a torch to light up the dark night. "As a member of the guard for the Kingdom of Calridian, I ask you again, who travels the mountain pass?"

With aid from the torch's light, Vurth was now able to identify the speaker of the group. Olvak stood in front with the torch held high. Olvak was a solid dwarf, who had taken to leadership quite well, and one whom Vurth trusted. "Very well," replied Vurth with fervor, "Olvak, you can consider your duty fulfilled. Well done! This is Vurth, your captain, along with Demorous on, an important errand."

All three dwarves hurried to salute their captain, as none of them had been able to identify who the travelers were that stood on the threshold of the light. After the salute, Olvak spoke again, his voice confident and conversational. "A pleasure to see you, captain. We had a feeling we might be seeing you soon. Let us have the honor of escorting you and Demorous the Fierce to the outpost."

"Seeing me? Did you even know I was awake from my uselessness," stammered Vurth.

"But of course; word traveled fast. Tagro made sure of it. The rest of the reason why you were expected will be explained in due time." Olvak paused a moment, noticing the fox for the first time. "What is this then?"

"All explained in due time," replied Vurth with a smile.

Olvak nodded in return before shifting his attention to the two dwarves beside him. "Come on now lads, let's lead our Captain to safety."

Another arc later saw the party of five enter the perimeter of the outpost. Small wooden fences had been set up in certain spots around the area. They didn't enclose the outpost in full but created cover and hiding positions in case the situation dictated the need. Vurth was happy with the response from those on the perimeter guard and the early warning they had given the main group at the outpost. Everything seemed to be operating as it should, and few things made a dwarf smile like a well-disciplined group of soldiers. That, drinking, and mining for minerals were about all there was on the shortlist. Many of the guards gave Vurth a salute or shout as he trotted by. Through it all the fox kept walking on, continuing to lead them somewhere. And it just so happened that the outpost was on the correct path.

When the small party reached the outpost building, Vurth and Demorous dismounted, leaving the horses in the care of Olvak. The outpost was a long wooden building with a tall wooden tower at one end. Vurth led Demorous up to the wooden doors leading into the outpost. Well, Vurth liked to think he did, but the darn fox was still in the lead. Two guards, one elf and one human, stood at the entrance. There were only a few humans in service to the king as guardsmen, so Vurth knew right away who it was. Vurth nodded to the young man and he knocked on the doors three times. A dwarf on the inside was quick to open the doors and gave his captain a salute as he walked by.

"I am sick of these salutes," grumbled Vurth as he walked in. "I never asked them to do it, but some of them do it anyway."

"Maybe they are just saluting the fox," laughed Demorous.

As if on cue, the fox ran down the long room to the end, where the Wanderer sat with two dwarves, laughing about something.

"Well, there he is." Vurth laughed out loud, filling the room with boisterous laughter. "That fox knew where he was going all right."

The Wanderer stood up and called to them. "Welcome my friends. I told you, Demorous, the fox would know what to do."

"That you did, though I don't know how." Demorous and Vurth walked over to the table and the two dwarves who had been talking with the Wanderer excused themselves.

"I didn't realize how fun your dwarves can be," commented the Wanderer.

"Aye, we can be. Now pour us two mugs of ale and tell us why we had to come all the way out here to find you," said Vurth, reaching for a half-full mug that one of the dwarves left behind.

"Because...I have news of the Bear's Heart."

The horde had not moved.

At two different times now, the horde had been dealt pain. Not something the creature ever remembered happening before. But now being touched by the lizard creature and a fall from a great height had injured the horde. The dragon had let go of its hold on the key and the horde fell. And fell. When it hit the ground its body spread out and stretched to its limit. This was after smacking a few trees on the way down.

As always one word was at the front of the horde's mind. Right now the word was rest.

So the horde stayed still, letting its body return to its normal shape. Rest.

16
Instrument of the King

Malick walked through the dark hallways of the castle, choosing to meet Mit in his quarters instead of the Throne Room. He hoped to surprise Mit, and in doing so, get the diplomat's true feelings about his time in Heritage. Malick had always been a supporter of Mit's. Gargan and Elonda had both shown disapproval in the past and now the king knew where those misgivings were coming from. Malick still thought he was a talented diplomat and hoped that this situation was just a misstep and not a total derailment.

Malick knocked on the door with gentle knuckles and waited for a response.

Mit called from the other side of the door, "Just a moment, please."

Malick didn't have to wait long before the wooden door was swung open. Mit was standing there with a smile on his face, about to utter a welcome. But his eyes went wide and his smile vanished in his surprise at the king being at his door. Mit stuttered, "Um...why... King Malick, to what do I owe the pleasure?" He then gave the king a quick bow and opened the door wide.

"Sorry for the unplanned visit, but may I come in?"

"Yes, of course, please come in." Mit gestured the king forward before closing the door behind them. Mit had no idea what the king would want from him, and only practiced discipline allowed him to stay calm in the unexpected situation. "How can I be of service?"

"There is something I feel I need to discuss with you," Malick paused, choosing his words with care. "I wanted to revisit the diplomatic mission to Heritage. I have a few follow-up questions if that is alright?"

Mit's heart skipped a beat. Again, only his experience in controlling his emotions saved him from displaying what would have been a dead giveaway to the king that something had made him uncomfortable. Why had this come up now? That had come and gone, and Mit had assumed that was put behind them. But all this he kept to himself and made a simple reply. "I would be happy to answer any questions you have, Sire."

"Excellent," Malick replied while gesturing to the small table and two chairs that were set up in the room. The wooden legs of the chairs rubbed on the floor as the two gentlemen pulled back the chairs to allow them to sit. "As we have discussed in the past, I know Jyres was a key to getting Heritage to join the Kingdom. Would you be able to expand on that for me?"

This was not going to end well. Mit ran his hand through his sandy-colored hair as he tried to sort through the possible responses. Somehow the king had now found out the truth behind the means Mit used to bring about the agreement with Heritage. It was the only explanation as to why the king would be bringing it up now. So either he had to come clean right away or play it off as something that was blown out of proportion. He decided to go with the latter.

"Oh, is this about that whole business about Jyres being from Heritage," smiled Mit. He chuckled, "It was a stretch perhaps, but no harm was done."

"What do you mean exactly?" Malick focused on Mit as he awaited an answer.

"You know how these things go, Sire, back and forth, give and take. Once there was a possibility of Jyres being from Heritage, it just kind of went from there. Nothing to worry about." There that should do it. Nothing to see here.

King Malick didn't seem to agree. "You are dancing around the problem, Mit. I can see through your words. It disappoints me. I had such high hopes." The king sighed and shook his head.

"Sire, I made the union happen," Mit spoke with a firm voice this time. "I was your instrument. You have a completed council and united kingdom because of me."

"I do. I agree," said Malick, looking at the ground for a moment before looking Mit in the eyes. "But what other corners are you willing to cut? What else would you sacrifice for your gain?

This time it was Mit shaking his head. "I get results, and I will continue to get results for you and this kingdom."

"I am unsure about that," said the king as he stood up. "I need to think on this conversation and consult with Advisor Esmeralda. We will decide together what role you will play for this kingdom in the future." The king then took his leave.

Mit Merrituk's anger built like a thunderstorm rolling across the plains of Alhazar. He stood in a hurry, the wooden chair clattering to the floor. He paced back and forth, the frustration evident. "Why now," he bellowed to the empty room. "What purpose does it serve? It was probably the she-elf, sticking her nose in other people's business. What gives her the right?"

Mit threw his hands in the air before kicking the chair that was still upright, only to hurt his foot. He screamed in frustration and pain before knocking that chair to the ground to join its partner. *Well, now what,* he thought to himself. It certainly looked like his place by the king's side was now in doubt. Maybe a walk to clear his head, yeah, a walk. Unsure why, he packed up the few things he called his own and, throwing the bag on his back, he ventured out of the castle.

Bluey and his band of misfits started after the group they had tried to surprise the night before. The sky today was a gray one, and what little sunlight had penetrated the cloud cover was now all but gone as the day waned. Their tracking led them to the Valley of the Dragons. From a safe distance away Bluey called a halt. He had no interest in following the click-clacks to Serenity Castle. He was known for taking risks but his survival skills told him that nothing good would come from venturing into the valley.

A low growl emanated from his throat. "We will have to find thems some other time. I want nothing to do with the Valley and its dragonsss." Bluey held the s on the end of "dragons" even longer, letting his disdain for the flying beasts show through.

"Yes, agrees," remarked one of his comrades. "But then whats do we do?"

Bluey looked around the area, taking in their surroundings. He made a show of looking in all directions, buying himself time until he thought of an answer. "What about Castle Mystic?" he finally said, pointing to the north.

"Whys there? Wizard place."

This brought a laugh to Bluey. Bluey was smart, this other goblin was not. "Wizard? Ha." Bluey laughed again. "The wizard is dead. It is a place for others now, a place for outcastss. Me thinks we can add to the group there."

"Whats about Ogla, click-clacks?" said the dumb goblin, and others seemed to agree with the question.

"Later!" Why did he have to explain everything? No, he didn't have to. "Because I said sso." Bluey motioned for the group to follow and they headed north, giving a wide berth to the valley. They were crossing the hills of Tomackus in the dark, something that few people did. In the past, as Vurth had discovered on one occasion, the goblins and orcs from the mountains would rush unsuspecting travelers. This had decreased significantly since the forming of the Council of Peace. It was also not something that this particular group would worry about. Bluey wasn't afraid of other goblins or their bigger relatives, orcs.

As the band of goblins reached the bottom of a hill they spotted a small fire that was lit and reflecting off the mountainside. Bluey put his finger to his lips asking for quiet and then led the way in between hills and bushes towards the campfire. Once they were a stone's throw away from the fire, the goblin leader again motioned to the rest, this time telling them to stay put.

Bluey surveyed the campfire and was surprised to see just one human male sitting there. The goblin scratched his head. It was rather odd to find lone travelers during the dark of night. He shrugged and, with care, he removed his long knife from his belt. Bluey crept toward the solitary figure by the fire. With one fluid motion, Bluey took the final step and wrapped his free arm around the human while he held his knife to the human's throat.

"Donts move. I think you would be smart to listen." Bluey held his knife a bit firmer to the man's neck to back up his statement.

"What is it that you hope to gain?" asked the man.

The man's voice was much too calm for the situation, and this bothered Bluey. He should be scared. Everyone is always scared of Bluey. "Your things, gold, now belong to uss."

The man chuckled. "Okay, well look around, I have very little in that regard."

What was going on? Why was the man acting so? "But you have a pack, a full pack I see."

"I do, you are correct. But unless you want a nice purple outfit for a human, I doubt you will find what you seek."

The rest of the goblins seeing Bluey had everything in hand, now approached. A couple of them came to stand next to Bluey, evil smiles on their faces, while a few others rummaged about the area looking for anything of use. They did, in fact, find the purple clothing Mit had referenced and threw it to the side. Bluey continued to grow frustrated as he watched his bandits come up empty in their search for something valuable.

"I guesss you were right, but that just means I kill you." Bluey hissed the words out, the intent in his voice evident.

"There is one thing here you have overlooked," remarked the still-calm man.

Bluey growled from deep in his chest. "Human! I grow tired of you!"

"Very well. Let me make it very clear for you." Mit cleared his throat. "My name is Mit. I am well known so others will come looking for me eventually. If you kill me, my guess is that you will have to deal with warriors from the Kingdom of Calridian. I am also guessing that is not the kind of attention you would like for yourself."

"We cans deal with that," Bluey started to apply more pressure with his knife on Mit's neck and a trickle of blood started to slide down his skin.

"Wait, wait..." Mit said, with a little more urgency. "I can also be of help to you. I have many skills. What is it you are trying to accomplish?"

Bluey held the blade where it was, not pushing anymore nor releasing any of the pressure. "Wes are heading to Castle Mystic, to add to our number."

"Excellent," responded Mit. "Diplomacy, recruitment, dealing with others, that is what I excel at. If you let me live, I guarantee you that I can make that happen for you."

Bluey thought about that for a moment, releasing the knife's pressure on the human as he did so. The goblins next to him turned to each other in surprise. "Bluey, whatss are you doing, kill him."

There are few things Bluey hated more than being told what to do. He turned on the goblins in an instant. "I decides what happens here. Not you. We need revenge on Ogla, on click-clack. We need more of usss. If he can do that, he has value. Like the human said."

Mit tried to take full advantage of the situation. "How many of you are there? 8, 10? I can double that number in one day at Castle Mystic." Mit, no longer with the knife at his throat turned to Bluey. "Give me a whole day at Castle Mystic. I will double your number. If not, then you kill me."

17
A Wizard in the Making

Cyna and Lumpkin once again found themselves in the makeshift apothecary, preparing for the spell that would not only duplicate the spike fragments but also retain the elements and composition of the original fragments. Lumpkin had the fragments separated from everything else and Cyna stood with Meslar's staff in hand. She took one more deep breath. "Ok, I am ready."

Lumpkin stood right next to the table. There he uncapped his duplication potion. He held it over the small shards of yixl spike and nodded to Cyna.

Cyna's nervous system began to send waves of anxiety throughout her body. They had practiced the spell many times, but now that the moment had arrived she didn't know if she had the courage to do it. She wiped the back of her hand over her sweaty face and took another deep breath. What was she thinking, she couldn't do this. She shook her head and her eyes met Lumpkin's.

"Yes. You can do it. Yes." Lumpkin nodded to her, imploring her to begin the spell.

Cyna raised her hands to her face and dragged them across it from top to bottom. "I can do this," she said aloud. And then before she lost any more confidence, she began reciting the words of power from the spell Lumpkin had taught her. She spoke with clear and accurate diction, holding tight to the staff...and the gem started to glow. Just as she finished speaking, Lumpkin let two drops fall onto the fragments. Almost instantaneous, another pile of spike shards appeared on the table. Cyna again felt that jolt of adrenaline and then that quick short wave of weakness.

It was Lumpkin's turn to take a deep breath as he again readied to drop the brown liquid on the brand-new pile of fragments. Lumpkin let the drop fall and watched in nervous anticipation as it landed on the pile. The dwarf was wrapped in disappointment for a moment as nothing happened. But then a puff of smoke sprang straight up from the shards. Lumpkin jumped with excitement. "It worked! Did it! We did it!"

Cyna smiled wide, joining in with Lumpkin's celebration. The two hugged each other, the reaction natural at first but it turned awkward in a hurry and they retreated to a safe distance. Lumpkin let out a sigh of satisfaction and clapped his hands together. "Well, more to do. Again. We must again."

Lumpkin now pushed the two piles together, combining the original and the duplicated fragments into one. And in so doing, doubling the amount. Once that was completed they repeated the process multiple times, creating more and more spike shards. Each time, the brown liquid produced that puff of smoke, which was the assurance that Lumpkin needed to feel confident that the process was working.

Each time, however, Cyna also felt that wave of weakness. And it seemed to be getting worse. "Lumpkin, I think this will have to be the last one. I am getting tired."

Lumpkin nodded his agreement and they repeated the process one last time. After pouring the duplication potion the dwarf looked up only to find Cyna wavering on her feet. Lumpkin was quick to come to her aid, but as he did so, the young girl collapsed.

"Cyna!" Lumpkin cried as she fell. He was able her to catch in his small arms, preventing her from banging her head against the hard floor. He lowered her the rest of the way down to the ground. "Cyna, okay? You okay?" he asked in a rush. He received no response and seeing that her eyes were closed tight, he ran to the door. He flew it open and shouted down the hall. "Help! Help, someone." Unsure of what else to do he returned to the girl's side.

Jyres rushed in a few moments later. "Cyna," he cried with alarm. He was by the girl's side in an instant. And with surprising heat in his voice, he turned to Lumpkin. "What did you do?"

Cyna woke in Jyres's arms. She blinked, blinked again, before smiling at her brother.

"You're awake," he said before lowering his hand to the side of her face. "You had me worried."

"I am okay now," she replied. Cyna reached up, placing her hand on top of his. "How long was I asleep?"

"Only for a moment." Jyres nodded in Lumpkin's direction. "I didn't even have time to find out what happened. You fainted is all." Jyres supported her as she sat up, holding onto her until he was certain she was able to sit. "Now, please tell me what happened."

Cyna nodded. Then thought better of it, as it sent a wave of dizziness through her. "Maybe Lumpkin can start," she commented.

Lumpkin started describing everything that he had been doing with his potions and the spikes but Jyres was having trouble following it all. But then Lumpkin mentioned the staff and Cyna's name and Jyres locked back in on the rambling dwarf.

"So. She used the staff and worked. Spell worked. We did it again, did it again, and then she.." the dwarf struggled to find the right words and ended on "fell over."

Jyres tried to hold his expression neutral as a myriad of thoughts and responses went through his mind. Instead of lashing out in anger at the dwarf, Jyres focused his attention back on his sister. Color seemed to have returned to her cheeks and her eyes no longer had a lost look to them. Jyres took a deep breath. Cyna would be all right. Whatever had happened here did not seem like it would have a lasting effect on her. "So, you used the staff multiple times?" he asked, looking at Cyna.

"I did. And at first, I felt a very quick tiredness that always went away. But then at the end, I guess it didn't go away. I am sorry if I worried you."

Jyres was already shaking his head. "You have nothing to be sorry about. How could you have known? Now you on the other hand.." Jyres turned on Lumpkin, the tone in his voice losing its patience. "You should have known better." Jyres pointed at the dwarf. "How could you let her go so far?"

Lumpkin took an involuntary step backward. "But... But...I didn't know. No. I... I..."

Jyres stepped towards him. "You are the more experienced one. You have been doing this for years, you were with Zar." Jyres took another threatening step toward Lumpkin.

"Jyres," Cyna said, standing up on her own. "Please, no, it is not his fault."

Lumpkin leaped at the opportunity. "Mistake, please, I mean no harm." He pointed at the staff. "Limited time. I have had staff limited time. Please, understand. Limited."

Jyres took a breath and let the frustration go with the exhale. It was wrong of him to take it out on the dwarf. He wasn't a delga wizard. Yes, he knew some things, and had lots of potions, but how would he know a young delga's limits? Limits that, in this case, had been exceeded. Jyres nodded. "Well, you are in need of rest, Cyna. Come, let's get you to your bed."

"Aye," said Vurth. "News of the Bear's Heart might make it worth the trip." Vurth took a swig of ale and focused his attention on the Wanderer.

"Yes, news." The wanderer stood up, then thinking better of it, sat back down to stay at the same level as the others. "I now firmly believe that the black donosin race used to be in possession of an item that could be what you referred to as the Bear's Heart."

Demorous rolled his eyes. "Really, you believe, that an item used to be... blah blah. How does that help us?"

The Wanderer lost his patience with his former fellow knight, not able to hold it in as he had done at their last discussion. "Seriously, Demorous! Give me a moment!"

The big knight threw up his hands in apology.

"As I communicated with the bears, they showed little response to the words the Bear's Heart. But it led me on the right path, trying to find something dear to them. They responded with a wave of emotion when I asked about anything that had been lost. More specifically, I believe they were in possession of an item that allowed them to speak as you and I do."

Vurth scratched his chin. "Wanderer, what are you saying?"

"What I am saying Vurth, and Demorous, is that we know the black donosin used to be able to speak. And, I know now that the donosin feel a deep empty hole from something lost in the past.

I believe the Bear's Heart is this thing that was lost, and that it is what gave them the ability to talk in the common language."

Vurth looked over at Demorous who shrugged. Vurth rolled his eyes in return before shifting his attention back to the Wanderer. Vurth looked the delga over. He was unsure of what to think about him and this story. Could he really "feel" what the bears were telling him? He had his doubts. But then again, he himself had seen the great black donosin act as a loyal dog in the presence of the Wanderer. Vurth shook his head, unsure of where to go next.

"I see you doubt my words," said the Wanderer. "But I have one more thing that backs up my theory. Demorous?"

"Yes," replied Demorous. "What is it?"

"Do you remember when last we spoke, I seemed..." the Wandered searched for the right word. He decided to go with, "distracted?"

"I remember. I had snuck up on you and you made vague references to something you had to investigate." Demorous stood up to stretch his back. "It wasn't anything I was going to understand."

The Wanderer nodded along with him. "Yes, correct. Well, the other thing the animals have been trying to tell me about is a change."

Vurth's doubts were starting to outweigh his confidence in this delga. "A change?" laughed the dwarf.

"Yes, a change," said the Wanderer a bit more stern than he intended. "Fewer and Fewer wolves have been seen in the old world. And...," the Wanderer continued before the dwarf and knight could express any more doubts. "That means that they are gathering somewhere, and rumors of dire wolves are circulating."

"Dire wolves," responded Vurth. "Have not heard of a dire wolf in an age. That seems far-fetched."

Demorous laughed. "Far-fetched? Like having three black donosin arrive at the castle? Or having four dragons instead of two? I think we have left the normal realm, and far-fetched is no longer 'far-fetched' my friend."

After a moment of silence, Vurth continued. "And, if there are fewer wolves, why does that mean they are gathering? Couldn't that have died off? Perhaps the dragons got hungry."

The Wanderer smiled at the dwarf's humor. "The numbers have changed too rapidly. Somehow, someone or something is gathering them."

"And you think this is all connected to the Bear's Heart?" Demorous asked. Demorous was still standing, and his left hand ran across his bald head. "It all seems...," the big delga didn't finish the thought. Just left it hanging in the air.

The three of them fell silent, each lost to their own thoughts. Vurth wondered if this could all be connected as the Wanderer said. A dire wolf? Really? Without a conscious decision, the dwarf pulled out his axe, placing its handle on the ground in front of him. He then spread his arms out over the top of the axe, leaning over it as he considered the line of thinking. Vurth's mind drifted back to the events of Meslar. He had gathered thars and orcs and goblins to his cause. Could something similar be happening here? And he still didn't understand what that had to do with the Bear's Heart. Was the Wanderer really so connected to the world around him as to be able to determine the situation he had laid out?

Vurth took another gulp of ale before returning the empty mug to the table. "Well, in the end, it probably doesn't matter what we think. Aye, Demorous? The king will have the last say."

Demorous just nodded and returned to his seat at the table.

"But," continued Vurth, "let's say all this is correct. And you Wanderer, are right about a gathering of wolves. We still don't know where they are gathering or where the Bear's Heart is."

"I felt a sense of concern when I mentioned the wolves to the black donosin. This means they have probably sensed them or know of them. Which means the search should start to the west of the gate." The Wanderer finished his mug of ale and set it back on the table with care.

"Fine... fine...," moaned the dwarf. "You have a theory for everything." After pausing a moment he said, "You are going to come and explain this all to the king."

The Wanderer smiled wide, "Oh, I thought I would get a head start looking for these wolves and let you take it back to him. You are a member of the Council of Peace, are you not?"

"Yes! He is!" shouted Demorous, who was already looking forward to the angst this would cause the dwarf.

"Thanks for nothing," Vurth grumbled.

Then, from out of nowhere, Mezzo the fox jumped up and into Demorous's lap. The fox was quick to curl up on the giant man's lap and then closed her eyes. There was a moment of silence before Vurth and the Wanderer both exploded with laughter. Vurth slapped his knee and almost fell out of his chair as the laughs continued.

On the outside, Demorous scowled at them and the fox. But on the inside... the fox was starting to grow on him.

19
Volunteers, Spears, and Fears

Bluey and his crew set up camp not far from Castle Mystic and he and Mit continued on to the castle. Castle Mystic had seen changes over recent years, but the outside of the castle was still dark and formidable. Lord Kapel had made an effort to ensure that the inside of the castle was not so bleak. Since the passing of Meslar and the disbanding of the Knights of Enchantment, Lord Kapel had tried to wash away the past of the castle by bringing about change for the better. The castle had become a home for those who had no home. Along with Lord Kapel, three other former knights also still called it their home. Felix, known for his speed, and the brothers Sigmon and Digmon. As it would happen, Felix was at the gate when Mit and Bluey arrived.

The gate was open but Felix stood alongside it, leaning against the castle wall. "A human and a goblin, that seems an odd pairing," he said as he stepped out in front of the gate.

"That it is, though not as odd as it once was." Mit's tone was light and in no way confrontational.

"Mr. Merrituk, I did not recognize you, what brings you here to Castle Mystic? And why the goblin companion?"

"Felix is it? Yes, just on a quick errand for the king and Council member Ogla." Mit smiled, hoping that Bluey was doing the same. In fact, Bluey was doing the opposite at the mention of the name Ogla. But Felix's attention remained on Mit.

"Yep, Felix it is. Fair enough. No offense, it's my job to ask questions," Felix stepped aside.

"Of course," said Mit, "Nice to see you again." Mit and Bluey then stepped past him and into the castle.

They were greeted with loud sounds from the citizens as they entered. The rooms and hallways closest to the castle gate had been turned into a market. People sold, traded, and bought goods from merchants, both from the castle and from those who had traveled to the castle to trade. Mit led Bluey away from the busy area, preferring a quieter section to do his work. *But,* he thought, *could he lose the goblin in the crowd*? Then he could make his escape after, or even hide in the castle for a while. For now, he decided to play it safe and stayed clear of the market.

Mit and Bluey stepped in through a doorway and into the main hall. Wooden tables and benches dominated most of the space, and most were open, with just a few people sitting in the hall. Mit made his way through the tables before approaching one such table that was occupied by two men. The man on the left was tall and lanky, and had a crooked nose. The man on the right had broad shoulders and a face that showed his age.

"May we join you?" asked Mit.

"It is a free castle," the skinny man replied.

Mit and Bluey sat down at the table and Mit began to try and engage the men in conversation. It was no easy task, but Mit found a topic they were interested in: sword making. The older man had been a blacksmith for a time, and Mit was able to keep the conversation going once he had discovered that tidbit. Eventually, Mit let the chatter die away and fell silent. But then once the older man asked him a question, beginning a new topic, Mit knew he had an opening. And he steered the conversation toward where it needed to go.

"Well, what do you think about going on a little adventure? Bluey and I are looking for a few more members for our crew?"

The skinny man just smiled and let the other man do the talking. "What's in it for us?" he asked.

That was a question that Mit didn't have an answer to, as he was not sure what Bluey had in mind. This caused a delay in Mit answering the question, leaving an opening for Bluey to talk.

"The spoilsss of battle, and the pleasure of victory," Bluey said, allowing a devious smile to show on his pale green face.

The man leaned back from the table. "I am a bit old for that kind of thing. This body isn't quite what it used to be."

This time Mit was ready with an answer. "We have the grunts for the hard work, we need experience and smarts."

This time the skinny one chimed in. "You must be after something?" His voice was hoarse and it came out as a rasp.

Mit held his finger up to Bluey, ensuring he didn't say anything. Up until this point Mit had just been trying to play it safe, get Bluey his guys, and move on. But now...now he was at an impasse. He had to say something. He knew. "Listen, my companion and I will talk a few things over and we will be right back." Mit nodded to the two men and motioned to Bluey. Mit and Bluey then walked to another table with no one in earshot.

"You promisssed me men," started Bluey. Throwing his arms up.

"Just give me a moment," replied Mit.

What was he going to do after this? He was frustrated with the king and saw little room to prosper there now. King Malick, just thinking of the name made his blood boil. He had given the king everything he wanted and now Mit was on the outside. Why? Because someone's feelings had gotten hurt? What a joke. No, there was nothing for him back at the castle. Which meant he was back at his first question. What was next?

Mit looked over to Bluey and saw the goblin struggling to hold his patience. Was there some sort of opportunity here with this thin, reckless goblin? Mit's hand moved to his chin as he rubbed the shaven hairs of his face. If not here, then where? Back to Skystair? Mit shook his head and rubbed his eyes. He didn't want to go backward, he wanted to move forward. He blew out a long breath.

"Bluey, you must have some sort of goal in mind?" Mit asked the question knowing the answer but wanting to see where it went.

"Yes, revenge, Ogla, Click-Clacks." Relief was visible all over Bluey that Mit had finally started talking again.

"Revenge." Mit smiled, thinking some revenge of his own would be fun. But revenge was not long-lasting. "Sure, but then what?"

Bluey just stared back at him with a blank expression.

Well, at least he knew what motivated the goblin. He could use that to his advantage, he was skilled in such tactics. The question was what would he leverage that advantage for? What was his motivation now? He wanted to be a man of influence. But he had to look outside of the kingdom for that now. And to have influence from the outside of the Council would also take a lot of power. Without a spot next to the king he would need something else to bring him the attention needed. He needed another way to wield influence on the kingdom. And...and suddenly he had a thought.

Smiling at Bluey he said. "I think I figured it out, let's go recruit some help."

And they did just that. Mit was more than capable and by the end of the day Mit had done what he had promised. More than what he had promised. 12 were recruited. The 12 included men, dwarfs, and a pair of female elves. Starting the next day they left in intervals so as to not arouse suspicion.

Altogether the group now numbered 24, including Mit and Bluey. It was a bit rocky for a moment or two as the new members realized the rest were all goblins. But Mit was able to keep everyone calm and by the end of the day, the group was heading into the mountains.

Lumpkin, Lalatco, and a few other elves and dwarves were in the depths of Castle Serenity. There they had begun to turn Lumpkin's and Cyna's growing collection of spike fragments into the heads of spears. Cyna and Lumpkin continued to work until they had enough material to work with. Jyres, however, was present every time they were working and insisted on frequent breaks for Cyna. Throughout the rest of the process, Cyna did not show any signs of weariness.

Now it was up to the skilled craftsman to turn the material into spears. The process involved melting the fragments and forming them into the spearhead shape. Lumpkin was fascinated by the process and enjoyed watching the elves and dwarves do their work. Lalatco had been assigned by the king to oversee the whole process. But other than a few suggestions here and there, he let the masters do their work.

For the wooden handles of the spears, they used a combination of crafting new handles and replacing the heads on spears they already had in the armory. All in all, Lalatco was happy with the progress and the process. There was only one problem. They had no idea if they would work. There were no guarantees that the spearheads would maintain the same properties throughout the magic and metalworking process. Lalatco had asked Lumpkin for his assurances, but even Lumpkin had his doubts. Lalatco shook his head before walking over to one of the elves who looked to be considering something.

Elonda, Cyna, and Jyres sat around a table in the main hall of the castle. They had just finished eating a nice meal during which Jyres made sure to avoid the topics of war, magic, and the like. But now that dinner was over, he took a deep breath, preparing himself for the conversation that needed to take place. King Malick had talked to him about Cyna and the Ring of the Seventeen. Malick had requested that Cyna begin preparations for learning the spell that would be needed to unmake the gate in case the time came when it was needed. Jyres did not like the idea at all. He had no way of knowing if that was something Cyna was capable of. And after she fainted during the duplication process, he had his doubts. But he also understood that she was the only delga they knew who had the capabilities to be a delga wizard. Putting all the pressure on Cyna, a girl of just 12, was unfair. Jyres knew what it felt like to have the fate of the world in his hands, and he would not wish that on anyone, especially his sister.

"Cyna," Jyres started. "We have something we need to discuss." Jyres had told Elonda earlier about this conversation and he knew he would need her to help guide him through it. He wasn't even sure what he wanted the outcome to be and right now he was not sure what to say next.

Elonda sensed his struggle. "It is important that you tell us how you actually feel about this okay, Cyna."

Cyna replied with a shrug, "Okay, sure."

Jyres started again. "The king has made a request of you. It is a pretty big one." Jyres paused making sure he had Cyna's full attention. "He has asked that you start to learn a spell that could help unmake the Gate of Fire."

Cyna was taken aback. "Me? The Gate of Fire! Is that even possible? Why would the king say that?"

"Well," Jyres struggled for the right way to explain it. "There is a very specific method, including races, positions around the gate, and a spell that can unmake the gate. And it requires a delga wizard."

Cyna scratched her head and for a moment touched her tight rows of hair. It was a nervous habit that she had started to do as of late. "But I am not a delga wizard."

Elonda placed her hand on the young girl's back. "We know you don't think of yourself as a delga wizard. But we do know that you are a delga, and we know you have cast a few spells. Spells that only a wizard could do."

"But that's just it, I only know two spells!" Cyna was starting to panic a little.

Jyres was quick to respond. "Take a deep breath, Sis, I know this is a lot." Jyres paused for a while, letting the words sink in and the shock subside. "The words for the spell are known and you wouldn't have to worry about anything else but the spell."

Cyna's hands went back to her hair. "Do you want me to do this?"

"I don't want to make this decision for you," said Jyres. But deep down he had no desire for Cyna to try this.

"Remember, Cyna," commented Elonda, "you need to tell us how you feel about what we are saying. What do you think about what the king has asked?"

"I just don't see how he thinks it is even possible," said Cyna in a voice so quiet, Jyres had to strain to hear it.

Jyres leaned back in his chair and looked over at Elonda hoping to snag her attention. But Elonda's focus remained on the young girl. Elonda was rubbing Cyna's back and talking in a quiet voice with her. Jyres let out a deep breath and stared up at the ceiling, letting his thoughts wander. But to his chagrin, he couldn't shake the sight of Cyna standing around the ring of fire with the fate of the kingdom resting on her.

A messenger saved him from his thoughts. Jyres took the messages from the man's outstretched hand. One said "Sands" on the outside and the other said "Elonda". Jyres handed Elonda hers and then unfolded the small parchment still in his hands. In dark ink across the top, it read, "Orders to the Sands family, from the Council of Peace."

Well, maybe it wouldn't be Cyna's decision after all.

Malick stood alone in the throne room. He felt cold and lost as dark thoughts swirled in his mind. Vurth and Demorous the Fierce had returned from their rendezvous with the Wanderer and Malick was not encouraged by what they had learned. He felt like they were grasping at any ideas at this point and everything had spiraled out of control. But they were out of time and out of ideas. Very late in the night, the Council of Peace decided on and put into motion their final attempt at avoiding what seemed inevitable: the return of those locked away, the horde.

20
Morning

The orders passed down to Jyres from the Council were what he had feared. The king had gone from asking, to ordering, in a short amount of time. Jyres was torn as to what to do. Cyna had been ordered to be a part of the Ring of Seventeen and to start memorizing the unmaking spell. Jyres, on the other hand, had been commanded to find the Bear's Heart. Jyres had delayed sharing the details of the orders with Cyna until he had had time to think it over. As much as Jyres wanted to disobey the orders and stay with Cyna, that would mean he would have to abandon his friends. Elonda, Lalatco, Leah, Vurth, and Gargan had all been given the same task. As had Demorous. They were to find the Bear's Heart and bring it to the Gate of Fire unless otherwise instructed.

The Council had decided to put all of their best assets on one team in an effort to find the Bear's Heart. It made sense to Jyres. A lot now depended on finding the artifact. Without it, there was no hope in casting the unmaking of the gate spell. Jyres was unsure of the other orders that were made and given out. But he knew the castle was a hive of activity that morning and many things had been set into motion. Although he was curious about everything that was occurring, in the end, it did not affect the decision that lay before him.

Jyres didn't know how he was supposed to go forward. Venture out with the love of his life and his friends to find an ancient relic. Or stay and be with his adopted sister and help her through what seemed like an impossible task. He knew that if he stayed with Cyna his friends would understand, and they would go on without him. How would he feel if something happened to them and he was not there to help? But on the other hand, how could he leave Cyna all alone? She had finally found someone she could count on, how could he leave her at a time like this?

Jyres had woken up early and, after readying himself, he went to the stables. He soon found that he was not the only one who had a morning ride in mind. Elonda was preparing her Wild Spirit when Jyres arrived. "Good morning," he said as he walked up to Gerti.

Jyres and Gerti had been separated for a while, but Elonda and the others at the castle had taken good care of his horse during his captivity. Jyres was excited to take her out for a ride, something he had been unable to do for quite some time.

"Couldn't sleep?" Elonda asked as she swung up onto her saddle, the black-colored horse now ready.

"Not all that well, but I was hoping to ride this morning anyway." Jyres finished preparing Gerti, double-checked the straps, and hopped up into the saddle.

The two riders eased the horses out of the stable, both having to duck to avoid hitting their heads. They were quiet at first, enjoying the changing colors of the sky as the sun greeted the world for a new day. It was a windy morning, which brought with it a chill that the sun had not yet forced away. Jyres, following Elonda's lead, increased Gerti's pace to a trot and soon they were leaving the valley.

"Where to?" asked Elonda who collected her long dark hair into a ponytail as she rode.

"Let's give the horses a workout, head to the hills." Jyres tried to smile, but Elonda could see right through him.

Elonda led the way and the horses galloped off toward the hills of Tomackus. "So, are we going to talk about it?" she asked.

"Not yet." Jyres knew he was just delaying the inevitable but wanted to enjoy the ride first. The two riders worked the horses up to a decent speed as the hills came closer. Jyres looked over to Elonda and smiled, before kicking Gerti and yelling, "Ya!"

It only took Elonda a moment to respond, letting Wild Spirit know it was time. Wild Spirit never needed much urging and closed the gap Gerti had initially created in no time at all. Then, as they approached the first hill, Wild Spirit's powerful legs drove him past Gerti and to the top of the hill. Wild Spirit was already down the hill as Gerti gained the top. Slowing the horses down the riders then brought them to a stop at the top of the next hill.

"You know you can't beat us," Elonda teased. "Even with a head start."

Jyres smiled wide. "I know, but we have to try. Don't we Gerti?" Jyres reached down and patted the horse on the neck. Jyres took in the sunrise and let out a deep breath. "I don't know what to do. I just don't see how I can make this decision. And for the king to put her in this situation..." Jyres's voice trailed off and he shook his head.

Elonda looked over at the man she loved. Although she felt many of the same things Jyres was saying, he was showing why she loved him. He was loyal and he would do anything for his friends. What seemed like so long ago now, when Jyres had gone with Lalatco on a journey to find Zar. Without really asking many questions, he had first taken a chance for his village, he passed through the ring of fire, and at the battle at Castle Serenity he had drawn Bram and his gargoyles away. He didn't do any of this for himself, it was all for those he loved. And now, he felt like he had to choose between her and Cyna.

The silence lingered a while longer before Elonda broke it. "Jyres, it is okay, you can stay here with Cyna." Elonda reached over and grabbed Jyres's hand. "Let us go find the Bear's Heart. You know we can do it." Elonda winked at Jyres.

Jyres smiled at her. "I know you can. But I would feel awful if something happened and I could have been there, done something."

"You don't always have to be the hero, you know. Didn't you learn that lesson at Heritage?" Elonda let go of Jyres's hand and let Wild Spirit trot around the crest of the hill.

Jyres watched the beautiful black horse as it pranced around on the grassy hilltop. "Trust me, I did. I know it takes all of us. Did you hear that, ALL of us. And if I am here and you are out there, that is not all of us. Plus, I need to see this thing through."

Elonda directed Wild Spirit back to where Gerti was, the horses facing each other, and Elonda pulled up alongside Jyres. Smiling, she said, "There is that hero talk again." Elonda leaned over and gave Jyres a kiss.

Every time she kissed him his heart soared. But despite Elonda's words, he had decided. "We are doing this together, I need to continue this path that I am on," Jyres said with a firm nod of his head.

Elonda was happy that he was going to be by her side, but she tried to hide her thoughts a bit, not wanting to sway him. "If it is any comfort, they can't perform a spell without the Bear's Heart. You can still be with her if it comes down to her saying the spell."

Jyres and Elonda turned the horses around, beginning the ride back to the castle. *That was true*, Jyres thought. He could still be there in the end when Cyna would need him most. He could be there for his friends and his sister. But it would still be a difficult conversation with Cyna, one that he was not looking forward to.

The horses entered the valley and slowed to a trot as they meandered along the river. When they were a little closer to the castle they spotted Cyna, Lumpkin, Kaleido, and Sunbeam all walking together towards the waterfall. The sight brought a small measure of comfort to Jyres. At least Cyna had a couple of dragons to look after her.

The closer the two morning riders came to the castle, the more activity they could spot. Servants of the king were moving all over and the stables were a hive of activity. Jyres and Elonda tried to stay out of everyone's way as they returned their mounts to the stable and moved on toward the waterfall to speak with Cyna.

"The four of you make an unlikely group," remarked Elonda as they approached Cyna, Lumpkin, and the two dragons.

Cyna turned away from the dragons and toward the familiar voice. "Oh, hi! I was wondering where you two were hiding."

"Not hiding," said Jyres. "Just...thinking."

Cyna laughed as Kaleido used his tail to splash water at her. "Always playing around," she remarked. Returning her attention to her brother, she asked him, "What were you thinking about?"

"Well," started Jyres, "you may have noticed that the king has made some decisions. And...well...those decisions don't have us going to the same spot. You and I, I mean."

Cyna's shoulders slumped a bit before she tried to shrug it off. "It's okay. Where are you going?"

"Well, we," Jyres motioned to Elonda, "are going to find the Bear's Heart."

Cyna thought about that for a moment. "So, what will I be doing?"

Elonda knelt in front of the young human and spoke in a soft voice. "The king would like you to continue to practice your magic and to start to learn that very important spell we talked about."

"I still don't know why he thinks I will be able to do this spell. I am still learning." Cyna shook her head and blew out a deep breath, keeping the tears at bay.

Jyres wrapped Cyna up in a hug. "I am hoping beyond hope that it doesn't come to that and that you will not have to try such a thing. But we need to be prepared. We may get to a point where we have no other options. But I will do everything I can to avoid that very thing." Jyres stepped back from her, put his hand on her shoulders, and looked her in the eyes. "And if it comes to that, I will be right by your side."

Elonda rested a hand on each of the Sands. "As soon as we find the Bear's Heart we will meet up with you. The spell can't be done without it."

Cyna nodded her head. "I understand. Please be safe."

"We will. Start practicing the words of the spell, stay busy, and we will be back before you know it," smiled Jyres.

"Don't worry about that, I've got these three to keep me company," Cyna motioned to the dragons and Lumpkin still playing by the water.

Elonda, Jyres, and Cyna then shared a long group hug.

21

Tracking

T he Wanderer knelt next to a game trail. The morning dew was damp on his knee as he inspected the ground. He had been following the trail of a wolf, but he had started to lose it in the rough and patchy ground. The footprints were large, bigger than what he was used to seeing. Despite the size of the prints, the terrain did not make for easy tacking. He was north of Stone Heights and had picked up the trail to the west of what was Bram's castle. He was about to give up the search when he found just the slightest mark of a footprint heading west.

The Wanderer looked around the area wondering where this beast would be going. If it went straight west it would come upon the dark rocky hills and spires that were directly south of the Gate of Fire. There was no guarantee that the wolf would continue in that direction, of course. Though, if it was going anywhere else it would have to change direction soon, for most creatures gave the ring of fire a wide berth and the Wanderer didn't see why the wolves would be any different.

The former knight closed his eyes, took a deep breath, and focused on the smells that the wind brought to him. As if he had called to the wind, a strong breeze blew past the delga. And with it a scent. It was a heavy smell, one of blood and death. It was coming from the west. The wanderer placed one hand on the ground and sent out his emotions to the wildlife around him and soon a few animals were drawn to him. A mouse scrambled across his hand

and a small bird landed on his shoulder. But then, a wild boar came nosing around, its snout touching the ground and sniffing. The boar looked up and saw the Wanderer. The boar was large and two tusks protruded from its face.

The boar stopped moving and gave a loud snort, and then one of its hooves pawed at the ground. Seeing this the Wanderer stood up, showing his full height to the animal. The boar snorted again and took a couple of steps closer. The Wanderer, not wanting to make any sudden movements, reached with painstaking slowness to his bone necklace. Placing his fingers on the bones, the Wanderer whispered a few words and took a cautious step toward the large animal. Seeing no reaction, the Wanderer took another step, and then another until he was within reaching distance of the boar.

The boar snorted again but made no other movements. With practiced motions, the Wanderer placed a hand right in front of the boar's snout. The animal sniffed the Wanderer's hand once, twice, and then took a step closer to the Wanderer. He placed his hand on top of the animal's head and moved to the side of the boar. The delga then patted the animal with both hands on its back, before throwing his right leg over the animal and straddling it like he would a horse.

The animal allowed him to and once he was seated the boar began walking toward the west and the unpleasant smell. The closer they got, the stronger the smell, and the boar seemed to want nothing to do with it. But it obeyed its rider for the most part and they continued their walk. The pair then came upon the source of the smell. In the middle of nowhere, laid a dead thar. The tall hairy creature was bloodied and disfigured. Despite his revulsion to the scene, the Wanderer slid off the boar and walked closer to get a good look. The thar was missing one arm, and teeth and claw marks were evident on the thar in many places. The Wanderer had little doubt that this was the work of the large wolf he had been tracking, and now he believed that the wolf he was tracking was a dire wolf.

Thars could be tough fighters in their own right, as Meslar had proved three years ago. So for a lone wolf to kill a thar with what looked like little effort, it had to have been a dire wolf. The Wanderer placed his hands on his waist and shook his head. This must have been what he was feeling those days earlier. Nature knew something was off; it was the dire wolves. Their presence had upset the balance.

The Wanderer circled the area looking for evidence of where the ferocious wolf went next. Finding the tracks, he called the boar over to him. The boar was hesitant to go anywhere near the thar. But with constant urging from the Wanderer, the boar worked his way over to where the Wanderer was standing, careful to avoid the mess that was the thar. With disgruntled noises, the boar shook his large head at the Wanderer.

"I know," the Wanderer stated as he mounted the wild board once again. "Unpleasant business." The Wanderer pointed into the west and the boar continued on. The Wanderer followed the tracks all the way to the base of the dark spires that stood south of the Gate of Fire. Once there, he dismounted from his temporary mount and surveyed his surroundings. The dire wolf did indeed appear to continue into the spires, but with the daylight waning, the Wanderer was not sure that he wanted to follow. If the spires were home to the dire wolf, he guessed that other wolves and/or dire wolves would be nearby. If so, a night investigation of the spires was a bad idea.

The Wanderer turned the boar toward the north and the spires located north of the Gate of Fire. The black donosins' lair was northwest of those spires, with some bears taking up residence in the black spires themselves. *Interesting*, the Wanderer thought, that both wolves and bears were in such proximity to each other.

But in reality, the gate and its ring of fire created an obstacle between the two locations putting more space between them than the distance shown.

The Wanderer skirted around the ring of fire, leaving plenty of distance between him and the ring. It was hard not to stare at the gate as he traveled across the open ground. It had stood there for so long. Untouched. And seemed to affect no one or no creature in any way. But not anymore. Things were coming to a head. Things were changing.

Karth, Simamar, three more elves, Rutu, and four other yixl had left the castle as soon as King Malick's orders had been dispersed. The group of ten had much traveling in front of them but hoped to move fast. Each yixl rode behind one of the others on a horse, but each horse had another horse tethered to it. This would allow the travelers to switch horses often and keep moving. Their goal? To track the horde, find it, and either capture it or kill it. Karth and the elves were all armed with the newly crafted spears and the yixl, of course, had their spikes.

The king was done with waiting and trying to extend their time. Multiple actions were underway. Karth, was of course, along to help with translation, and the king had appointed Simamar, his nephew, to lead this very important mission. The king had also kept two yixl at the castle, making sure that they didn't put all of their eggs in one basket.

At first, Simamar's only concern was speed. They ran the horses hard, switching often, and hoping to arrive at the mountain pass outpost in record time. Simamar put his faith in the patrols of the mountain pass and showed little concern for safety or caution. But the risk was rewarded and the first part of the journey went very well.

In the days that followed, the group traveled through the mountains and presently entered the forest in the Stone Way. Now that they were traveling in the old world, Simamar slowed the group and started to use caution. Something that did not come naturally to the elf. He had a much more aggressive nature and an eagerness to please the king. But his caution would also be rewarded.

As the group of ten traveled through the forest they soon realized that they were not alone. Another group was traveling to their northwest. Either the group was much larger or just didn't care if they were being heard. Simamar and the other elves could hear them as if they were right next to them. And even the yixl could hear them, despite not having hearing as attuned as the elves. Simamar motioned for the group to come to a halt and to remain quiet. He then selected another elf to accompany him and the two of them went off to investigate.

The two elves were careful not to make noise as they approached the other group. Each step was placed with care, as they paid attention to the branches, wanting to avoid as many of the bigger ones as possible. With each passing moment they came closer to their quarry, and before long the two elves stopped their progress and settled in among the undergrowth to hide themselves from the approaching group.

The two spies did not have to wait long before the loud travelers were passing by. Simamar had to fight to stay still as he saw who passed by his hiding place. Not more than a few arms lengths away walked Mit Merrituk. And alongside him, and behind him, marched a surprising mix of races. Humans, elves, orcs, and goblins all walked and stomped their way past Simamar and his fellow elf. Simamar's gaze flashed back and forth looking for any other details that would help him understand this interesting turn of events, but he came up empty.

After he was sure enough time had passed and the voices of the mixed group were far away, Simamar motioned to his fellow spy and the two of them began to make their way back to where they had left their group. As they did so, Simamar's mind raced. What was Mit doing out here? And with such an interesting group of companions? Did the king send him on some mission? Simamar had no idea. And in truth, it mattered little. He was assigned to find the horde, so that was where his focus would remain.

The horde had lost all sense of time and feeling. It remembered falling before slamming into the ground. In response, the horde's body flattened out to absorb the force. The horde felt so thin, never before had it been stretched in such a way. He wondered how much further he could have fallen. Could he have survived a fall from any height?

Twice now the horde had experienced pain. First by the creature with spikes, and now from the falling from such a great height. As the horde lay on the ground he could feel his body recovering, restoring itself to its natural shape. The horde had no idea how long it had been there, but he knew now that it would not be long until his body was ready. He turned his head just enough to see the key still stuck in his palm. The horde hissed. It was time for his brethren to be free.

The horde were always at their strongest when they were to-gether as a group. As individuals, they still could hurt or even kill. But their minds worked as one. Separate, they didn't have the mind power for strategic thinking or even accurate assessments of situations. Hence the horde had seen Bram and the Silver Shadow as a way around that weakness. But now. Now with the key in its hand, the horde could almost hear the voices of the hundreds locked away in another realm. Release us. Release us.

22
The Search for the Bear's Heart

It had been a few arcs into the day before Jyres, Elonda, Lalatco, Leah, Vurth, Demorous, and his devoted fox had left Serenity Castle. This small but mighty group left on foot, traveling as light as possible. They only carried weapons and the needed food and water. At night they planned on getting rides from Gargan and other gargoyles, which would decrease the travel time. But until then, they planned to travel as far as they could.

Cyna had seen them off as had Tagro. It was not easy by any stretch of the imagination for Jyres to leave her behind. But Cyna had put on a strong face and held her tears in check, which at least made it bearable. Vurth and Tagro clasped arms and talked to each other in low voices, sharing a private moment between father and son. Vurth then slapped him on the shoulders while Cyna gave a tight hug to both Jyres and Elonda. Then they were off and Cyna and Tagro stood watching them go until they were out of sight.

Attempting to keep Jyres's mind from his sister, Elonda spoke up. "Well, where do we start looking for the Bear's Heart?"

Vurth was the one to respond and his voice from the back of the group carried to the front with ease. "The Wanderer is supposed to be finding that out as we speak."

Elonda nodded. "Yes, and what if he doesn't have any information for us?"

Vurth barked out a short laugh. "I reckon he will. Something odd about that delga, I am not sure what it is. But I decided that I wouldn't doubt him when it comes to this kind of thing."

Demorous, always looking to pick a fight with the brash dwarf, said "And when would you doubt him?"

Vurth smiled, "perhaps if he had to fight me for some reason or any other dwarf with an axe,"

Demorous, "I will take that bet. Your swing couldn't even reach his shoulders."

Vurth huffed. "I will show..." But the rest of his comment was drowned out by Jyres and Lalatco. In unison, they shouted out. "Leave it!" Then Jyres followed it up with, "You guys would be arguing about that for half the trip, so let's leave it alone."

"Yes, let's," Lalatco and Leah agreed.

When night had fallen, so had the cold, making it the coldest night of the fall up to this point. The group's aerial rides soon arrived and Gargan and his fellow gargoyles swooped down to the mountain pass and landed. After an exchange of pleasantries, each traveler climbed on the back of a gargoyle and, with Jyres and Gargan in the lead, the gargoyles climbed the side of the mountain pass and jumped into the wind once they had reached an acceptable height.

Once they were above the mountains and in the even colder air, Jyres took a moment to appreciate the view. This was something Jyres had grown accustomed to. The others with him had varying experiences with flying, either with dragons or gargoyles, and Jyres could only imagine the look on Vurth's face. They traveled well into the night and all of the travelers were tired and chilled to the bone when the gargoyles landed to let their companions rest.

The group alternated between walking, flying, and sleeping as they made their way across the mountains and into the old world and then on from there looking for the Wanderer. Jyres, Elonda,

Lalatco, Leah, Vurth and Demorous all felt a little out of place when they stopped for the night at Bram's old castle. With the gargoyle clans now aligned, it made sense. But it still seemed odd. Jyres and the others had fought against Demorous and the knights in this place. And long had it been the home of an enemy of Gargan. But Gargan assured them all would be alright.

And all was. In fact, Jyres and his friends enjoyed a much-needed rest. It was later in the day before they set out again from the castle. Gargan and the many other gargoyles were still in their stone shape, but Jyres knew that, as always, Gargan would soon come gliding after them. The small group set out and not long after they had left, met with the Wanderer west of what had been Bram's castle.

After the exchange of greetings, Vurth didn't waste any time. "So, what have your wanderings found for us?"

"Always right to the point," commented the Wanderer, who gestured with his head to the southwest. "I followed a dire wolf to those dark spires."

Jyres spoke next, "A dire wolf, you are certain?"

"I am afraid so. I tracked it for much of a day. It took care of a thar with no issue. It was a dire wolf, of that I have no doubt."

"This supports your theories," said Demorous. "Perhaps there is a connection, as you say."

Lalatco had moved on from the group a little, taking in the area, watching with his far-seeing eyes. Calling back to the group he said. "There is evil on the wind. I can feel it."

"Oh, for the sake of the mountains!" (a common dwarven phrase) shouted Vurth. "Not you too! One crazy nature mystic is enough, we can't have you joining them."

This brought laughter to the group as Lalatco joined their circle again. The Wanderer put his arm around the warrior elf's shoulders and smiled back at the dwarf. Vurth rolled his eyes and shook his head. "I give up. Point me in the right direction, my axe is hungry."

Restoring order to the conversation, Jyres asked, "Do you know how many wolves there are? Or where there are gathering?"

"I am almost certain they are in or near those dark spires. Unfortunately, I only saw evidence of the one wolf. I tracked him for most of the day, but didn't think it wise to venture into those spires alone in the dark."

"We can't fault you for that," said Demorous.

"No, not at all," agreed Jyres. "The king will have need of a few of the black donosin. Please organize a group of them to meet us at the gate."

"I assumed as much. That I can do." The Wanderer paused. "I don't know that I am in support of you going in unprepared and outnumbered to a den of wolves."

Elonda smiled and looked the Wanderer in the eye. "You don't know much about us do you?" she teased. "This group is never unprepared and has never fought a battle we cannot win."

In response, they all clapped each other on the shoulders, forming a tight half-circle around the Wanderer, with even Demorous joining in on the bonding.

"We will be fine," said Jyres, looking at each of his friends in turn before returning his attention to the Wanderer. "Just have those black donosin by the gate. And watch for others coming from the new world to prepare the Ring of the Seventeen."

"Very well," sighed the Wanderer. "Good luck to you." The Wanderer shook each of their hands in turn, saving his former brother-in-arms for last. "Take care of yourself."

Demorous nodded and watched as the Wanderer headed off to the northwest.

The small but mighty band set out again, this time in the direction of the black spires. They stayed alert as they marched on,

Lalatco more often than not leading the way with Vurth bringing up the rear. The day dragged on and the conversation died off, each retreating to their own thoughts. It took the night, and another day, before the group neared the spires.

Jyres and Lalatco chatted and decided the group would make camp at the base of the southernmost black spire. So the group walked on, trusting their senses as the sunset took the light away from the world for the night. Upon reaching their destination, Lalatco and Elonda started to scout the immediate area while the others set up camp. Feeling the area was safe for the moment, the two elves returned to camp not long after a fire had been started. Although the air was cool, the fire filled the camp with warmth. Pockets of conversation started, as Elonda and Leah chatted about something and Vurth talked to himself as he got comfortable. Jyres stood by Lalatco who peered into the darkness.

"What is it?" Jyres squinted into the distance knowing full well he wasn't going to see whatever it was his friend had spied.

"I am pretty sure it is Gargan coming to join us. But we have had a few bad run-ins with gargoyles and, it is hard to remember that no matter who it is, they are on our side now." Lalatco turned to look at the dark spires that pierced the sky behind him. "Not much to look at are they?"

"Ask me again in the morning...all I see are silhouettes."

A short time later, Lalatco was proven right as Gargan swooped down from the sky and joined the group by the fire. Jyres filled Gargan in on what the Wanderer had said and the conversation died off after that. Jyres looked around the circle. He smiled at Elonda who was next to him and she rested her head on his shoulder. Vurth's eyes seemed to be getting heavy and Lalatco and Gargan were in a quiet conversation. Leah sat next to Lalatco, listening, while Demorous seemed to be wrapped up in his thoughts as he stared at the fire. For some reason, the sight of all his friends around the fire brought a memory back to him.

"Lalatco or Leah, do you remember that song Zar sang to us that night around the campfire?" Jyres smiled at the memory.

Lalatco turned toward his friend. "That is a great comparison to our current situation," the elf grinned at the thought. "But I can't remember the words."

"A Journey We Here Have Begun?" asked Leah. "I know it well." And without prompting she started to sing the upbeat song. That was all Jyres and Lalatco needed to remember it and they joined in while the others sat back and listened.

After the song was over, Jyres smiled wide. "I do miss that old man."

"Me, too," said Leah, who, after Jyres, probably knew Zar the best. She turned to her husband. "Lalatco, sing a song for us; one that we have not heard before."

Lalatco tried to shrug it away, but everyone knew he would sing. Because he loved to sing, but in large part because he would do anything for his dear Leah.

Lalatco stood up and took a step closer to the fire. He gazed into it, getting lost in the flames. Just when everyone else was wondering what he was doing he started to speak. "I think I have the perfect song, but I do require a partner."

Shaking heads and murmurs of "no, thanks" were heard around the circle. Lalatco's singing ability was all but unmatched and no one had the confidence to join him in whatever he was thinking. "Elonda, you know this song, please join me."

Reluctant at first, Elonda fidgeted, but the cheering and encouragement from her friends got her to her feet. She had a feeling she knew what song was coming. As long as Lalatco gave her the shorter part she could manage. She stood across from him on the other side of the fire. Lalatco smiled at her and she nodded.

The first words and notes flowed like sweet wine from his mouth. Elonda recognized it right away as the song she was expecting. It was a song from another time, one that had been passed down through the ages. It was about two long-lost friends, who, despite the distance, stayed connected. It was a song Lalatco had sung for her long ago, before they were just friends and when they might have been something more. As they sang-and to her relief-she had the easier part, she found it meant even more to her now than it did back then.

Where have you been my long-lost friend
Where have you gone I cannot find you
When will I see
When will I see

I am right here my forever friend
I know you can't see me, but I am here

It has been so long too long my friend
When can I hear you please come near
When will I hear
When will I hear

If you listen close you will hear
My voice will carry to wherever you are

Come close, so I feel your strength
The night comes and takes away the chance
When will I feel
When will I feel

THE RING OF THE SEVENTEEN

I reach for you through the night
Take my hand and hold it fast

When was the last time I heard your song
You are the one who lifts me up
When will you sing
When will you sing

I sing for you every night my friend
I sing for you now just listen close

I see you now my long-lost friend
I do hear your voice its sweet sound
Now I will see
Now I will hear

I knew that you would my friend
It is as I told you it was

I can feel your presence now so close
I hear the sweet melody of your song
Now I will feel
And now you sing

My friendship has been and is always here
Distance has no meaning here.

Elonda struggled to finish her two lines of the song, fighting through her tears. As soon as it was over she ran over and gave Lalatco, her long-time friend, a hug. It was an embrace of pure friendship and remembrance. After the hug, Elonda looked around and there wasn't a dry eye in the camp. Jyres and Leah joined

Lalatco and Elonda in their hugs and soon the tears of joy turned to laughter. Gargan chose that moment to make his presence felt and scooped all four of them up in his large arms, picking them up off the ground as he did so.

Jyres saw Vurth wiping his eyes and while he was being hugged by the giant gargoyle he shouted, "Vurth, are you crying? The mighty dwarf has tears."

"No, no, just got something in my eye," the dwarf lied.

Demorous the Fierce took this all in. He could not deny it. The elf's talents for singing and for the dramatic are unmatched. Demorous didn't have quite the same friendship, perhaps, as the others had. His start with them had been rocky and Meslar's stain still lingered in some ways. But even still, he, too, was touched by the song. He looked on as the others gave hugs and laughed through the emotions of it all. He reached down, scooped up his fox, and petted it as it got comfortable in his lap. Vurth nodded in his direction as the dwarf walked over to his friends. Demorous nodded in return.

23
Preparation

K ing Malick sat down with a groan. He had just sent Tagro off to make the final preparations for the assembled army to march. It took a lot of planning and supplies to move so many warriors. This was something that Vurth would have planned under normal circumstances, but this was by no means normal and Vurth was already gone along with Jyres and the others. Malick just hoped Tagro, Son of Vurth, was up to the challenge.

The door opened at the far end of the hall and Lord Kapel entered. Kapel held a large parchment in one hand and approached the king without hesitation. "I have it ready," he said as he untied the yarn holding the parchment in a roll. He unrolled the parchment on a large wooden table near the throne and the king came to stand by him. "I know you have been waiting for this, and I do apologize for the delay, but such things must be done right. Nor can they be rushed."

The parchment that was now displayed on the table was a diagram of the ring of fire. The dark black ink was thick and bold and the markings and notes were detailed and done by a steady hand. The king looked it over, inspecting the work. "This is well done," he commented as his gaze moved back and forth across the pictures and writings.

"Thank you, sire," responded Lord Kapel, who also stared down at his work.

Both of them stood silent awhile as they studied the design. It depicted the ring of fire and the Seventeen that would need to be stationed around it with the exact specifications that the unmaking spell had required. The king was more than satisfied with Lord Kapel's work. This was exactly what he was hoping for, and would make the next steps much easier. "This is obviously the Bear's Heart location here," the king said while pointing to the diagram.

"Quite right," said Lord Kapel. "And here, on the exact opposite side is, where the delga wizard needs to be." Kapel's outstretched finger showed the king the spot. "You will notice, I took the liberty of adding Cyna's name, just here. I have left the other spots blank, but my quill is ready with your order."

The king smiled. Cupping his chin in his hand, he considered the diagram before him. He was appreciative of the delga standing beside him, whose gift of intelligence had proven quite useful, both now with this diagram and in recent days. *It was a remarkable thing, really*, thought Malick. For not long ago he had had his doubts about the trustworthiness of any of the knights. Because of their former alignment with Meslar, of course, and then again with the Silver Shadow's recent exploits. But he was putting much trust in Lord Kapel about matters of ultimate importance to the Kingdom of Calridian. Returning his attention to the matter at hand, he turned to the delga. "Where should we start?"

"Might I suggest starting with the triangle," Lord Kapel motioned toward the diagram again. "You will see a triangle marked in each spot where they are needed. Two letters alongside denote whether it is a donosin, a dragon, or a delga. Have you heard from the Wanderer?"

"Yes, he will have donosin there. We must trust he can send them to the locations we specify. So let's look at the dragons and delga.

I want Esmeralda positioned nearest Cyna and Crimson near the Bear's Heart."

"Very good," replied Lord Kapel who readied his ink and quill and began writing the two dragons' names in the spots specified by the scroll and the king. When he was done with both names he looked back to King Malick. "And one more dragon is needed."

"Yes, we will let Esmeralda decide which one it will be. The other young dragon will stay with Cyna." The king paused. "For the delga, I will defer to you."

"Am I to assume that Demorous and Karth are not an option? Or did you have other plans?" To Lord Kapel's thinking, the odds were much more in their favor if they controlled what they could since so much of this was not possible to be planned. But he wasn't the king, so he did not want to assume anything.

Malick thought things over for a moment. "I don't think we can include anyone in Jyres's group or Simamar's as an option. We have no idea which of them, if any, will return to us on time."

"Agreed," Lord Kapel scratched his chin; it was his turn to ponder. After a pause, he said, "I will suggest Felix, the Wanderer, and myself. That would leave Brigand and his healing ability available for you to position as you choose."

"I am surprised you would suggest yourself. Shouldn't you be available to ensure everyone is in the correct place?"

Lord Kapel had expected this reply and nodded along with the king. "Once they are in their positions there will be nothing left for me to do. I feel like I am better suited for this role. Sigmon and Digmon are warriors and you can send them into battle."

"Very well, proceed," said the king, resigned to the fact that no decision would be an easy one, and when it came to the delga, he would trust Lord Kapel.

Kapel wrote in the names, his quill slow and deliberate, and more of the bold ink was added to the diagram. When he was done he stretched his back, and said, "Now, we just need to decide on the six other races."

"Right." The king clasped his hands behind his back as he considered. "As stated before, we have the six needed. Elf, dwarf, human, yixl, gargoyle and orc."

"Agreed, with one correction. That assumes we would attempt this during the night. If it is daytime, we would be short by a race."

The king hadn't thought about that. Kapel was right, of course, gargoyles were solid stone during the day. "Do we know of other races? At this stage, I have my doubts?"

"Other races? Depends on what the spell recognizes as a race. Dire wolves? Are goblins the same race as orcs? Shepherds of the Isles same as humans? Would a stone gargoyle in the right spot still count as one of the six races?"

That was another good question, and Malick thanked whatever circumstances had brought Lord Kapel to be standing here with him. They both stood in silence for a time and then Malick began pacing the room, his thoughts full of questions. Before long, he came to a stop back by the delga and the diagram. "For now, we go with the philosophy that a stone gargoyle is still a gargoyle. Gargan is of course after the Bear's Heart, but both Percy and Hawkins will be available to us. And perhaps we need to arrange to have a backup available to us."

"That is smart; control what we can. And in that case, we shall keep Sigmon and Digmon close to myself and the Wanderer. I trust Felix's skill and speed." Lord Kapel added more names to the diagram, including Hawkins and Percy.

"For elf, it will be me," said the king. "And I will not hear otherwise. I have more motivation than anyone else, and perhaps more skill. I will have a couple of elves from the guard with me. For dwarf, we will have Tagro, and other dwarven soldiers as a backup.

For yixl, we have a few left with us. Orc will be Ogla and anyone else he brings with him. That just leaves a human."

Lord Kapel's quill was busy marking down all the names the king just listed off. As he worked, he replied to the king. "Jyres and Leah are not options but perhaps the most trusted humans we know. Who else do we consider?"

Malick had to think about that. He wasn't sure. But as he considered, one name came to his mind and stayed there. "Shepherd Rowland."

"A solid choice, though you have his age to consider."

"He is the right choice," replied the king.

"Right choice for what?" came a raspy voice from behind them.

The king and Lord Kapel had been so engulfed in their task that they hadn't heard Shepherd come in. Turning in surprise to him, Malick said, "You shouldn't sneak up on your king like that."

"Trust me, no one has used the term sneaky with me, ever," the human laughed.

"Well," said Lord Kapel, "we need a human to stand in our Ring of Seventeen."

"Then you are correct, I am the right choice. I have some fighting spirit left in me."

Malick nodded. "Then it is all settled. The plan is ready. Let us hope we don't have to unleash the spell when we have no idea what will result."

24
The Dark Spires

The morning sun had already lit up the world by the time Jyres and the small group started to pack up camp. Gargan stood as solid stone.

Lalatco walked over to Jyres, who was looking up at the dark spires before them. "So, not much to look at are they?" asked Lalatco, repeating his question from the night before.

Jyres thought about that for a moment. The spires rose up like rocky spikes reaching for the sky. Not quite mountains, but taller and more intimidating than hills. "Well," Jyres commented, "I am not looking forward to climbing them if that is what you mean."

When the group was ready, they gathered around. "So...what's the goal?" asked Leah.

"We are assuming the wolves are hiding somewhere in these inviting rocks behind us," said Jyres. "Let's scout around, but stay together, I don't like the idea of someone finding the lair on their own."

"Agreed. But if we can manage to find them without giving ourselves away, that will give us the advantage," said Demorous.

"And I would much prefer to confront the wolves with Gargan at our side," remarked Elonda.

Jyres thought about that for a few moments before coming to a decision. "Let's scout in groups of three. Hopefully, that achieves both objectives. Elonda and Vurth will stick with me. Demorous, you will go with Lalatco and Leah." The others nodded their agreement and Jyres added. "But plan on meeting back here in three arcs time to report."

"I like that idea, but maybe we can find a good meeting place higher and further into the spires. That will keep us from backtracking too much. We can stick together until we find a suitable spot," said Lalatco.

With the plan finalized the six adventurers began their trek into the spires. At first, the going was easy enough, but the terrain got rockier and steeper as time went on. Lalatco was in the lead and after about an arc into their travels he called a stop on a natural overlook. The view was to the east and back toward where they had camped the night before. "This should do," said the elf once everyone had joined him. "Let's make this our rendezvous point."

"Great," Jyres confirmed. "We will see you back here in three arcs. Be careful."

Jyres, Elonda, and Vurth let the other three leave first, taking a rocky trail that descended a bit and branched to the north. Jyres led the other two to the west. It became more difficult to remain silent with every step, as loose rocks and pebbles seemed to scatter every time you moved your foot. A short while later the three of them stopped at a point where no obvious path was evident.

"Well, now what?" Vurth was not in a great mood after all this climbing. "I am not trying to go that way," Vurth pointed to the west. "No way we can climb that. And we are making too much noise as it is."

Jyres had to admit, Vurth was right. He didn't see a way to keep moving forward. And as much as it seemed like a waste of time, they were going to have to backtrack. Jyres, shaking his head in frustration, motioned for the others to follow him, as they retraced their steps. They trudged almost all the way back to the natural overlook before they found another possible path for them to follow. To the group's dismay, the next couple of arcs didn't prove much more productive and they found themselves back at the overlook, waiting for Lalatco, Leah, and Demorous and their report.

Lalatco, Leah, and Demorous, at first, didn't fare much better. But then Lalatco found a natural trail that ran between spires. The trail didn't have significant elevation changes and allowed the travelers to move with more stealth. After a good part of an arc, the path ran into the base of multiple spires ahead of them, ending the easier terrain. As the group assessed which way to try next, they heard an unmistakable wolf's howl that sounded like it came from just on the other side of the spires that stood tall next to them. Lalatco motioned for the other two to remain quiet, and the three of them waited to see what would happen next. Not wanting to make noise, they stayed in that location for what seemed like forever to the three travelers. Having to be quiet just seemed to make the arc go by with painstaking slowness.

When the noises from the nearby wolves got further and further away, only then did the group decide it was okay to talk again. They agreed that too much time had passed to continue the search and headed back toward the natural overlook to meet up with the other half of their group.

Once everyone was back together, they shared their findings. After a few quiet moments passed between the group, Elonda broke the silence. "Maybe we are going about this all wrong."

This drew the attention of her friends. "What do you mean?" Jyres voiced the question that they all were thinking.

"Well. The wolves obviously need a path in and out of these rocks. I don't see them going up and down all over the spires like we have been. According to the Wanderer, these dire wolves are large, and I don't see them taking the paths we have been on today."

"I agree," said Leah, looking to her husband to hear his thoughts.

"I do as well. But we did find one path that certainly could allow wolves to travel, so there are options for them. Not sure how else we should proceed. But what were you thinking, Elonda?"

Elonda shrugged, one of her hands pulling her ponytail in front of her mouth as she pondered. Throwing her hair behind her again, she said, "Maybe we just start lower. Walk around the base until there is a more obvious path."

As the conversation continued Vurth and Demorous stepped away from the group and began to organize camp. The fox followed along. It didn't take long, as they had packed light, but darkness was coming and they wanted to make sure all was in order.

"Well, I don't think we will accomplish anything more tonight," sighed Jyres. "I don't think it is smart to be wandering around in the darkness with wolves nearby."

Vurth heard the comment and replied as he positioned wood for a fire. "It's probably not a whole lot smarter to be sitting in one place for them either."

Jyres smiled and then nodded. Vurth was right, as well. Neither option was ideal.

Lalatco responded. "This is a good spot to camp. They can only come at us from one direction." The elf walked around the area and pointed as he talked, emphasizing his thoughts. "Plus, the rocks pinch the possible paths in that direction. We should be safe here."

"Safe enough for a fire?" Vurth questioned leaning over the wood and about to start the flames.

"Gargan needs to find us anyway," said Jyres. "Go ahead, it will get cold otherwise."

With the approval, Vurth started the fire with a spark from his rocks, and soon the fire gave off its warming heat. Not long after that, Gargan swooped down from the sky and landed on the small outcropping. They all exchanged greetings before Jyres gave Gargan a quick update on the day.

"I see," the big creature replied. "I already have many gargoyles patrolling this area." Gargan pointed to the sky as he talked, and the group could spot other gargoyles in the sky. "I will spread the word for them to watch for any wolves leaving or entering the spires. Maybe one of them will spy a wolf. I can also have one of my brethren camp here with us. That way the two of us can keep watch and all of you can rest."

This did not cause any argument as his friends were thankful for the possible night of restful sleep. Gargan left for a moment but returned after connecting with one of his followers in the sky and relaying the instructions. Soon, another gargoyle joined them by the fire and the others settled down the best they could on the hard ground. Despite the less-than-ideal circumstances, tiredness overcame being uncomfortable and worried and most were sound asleep in half an arc or less. Jyres took the longest to fall asleep, but once he moved to be as close to Elonda as the situation allowed, he soon joined the others in their slumber.

Gargan and his fellow gargoyle spent most of the time in silence, with an occasional conversation. Other gargoyles often landed at the camp to give reports to their clan leader. As the night wore on, wolves were spotted a few times by the gargoyles from overhead, but through their observations alone they were unable to ascertain a specific path for the wolves. Right before the sun came up, Gargan woke Jyres to report the information.

In the morning, the group decided to stay together, thinking they wanted to avoid too much distance between the two groups. After reflecting on last night's conversation, they started where Lalatco's group had left off the night before. That was the only path that had shown any signs of wolves. Gargan and his friend were statues, left like stone guards around the old campfire. Lalatco lead the group, following their steps from last night. Once they arrived at the open path, he slowed the group down and used caution, but that seemed unnecessary as no wolves made themselves known.

"Fan out," said the warrior elf. "Look for tracks or other signs of passage."

The others did as they were asked, searching the ground for tracks and listening for any nearby animals. After some time, Vurth's and Demorous's search efforts became lazy, and before long the others seemed to give up as well.

"Now what?" asked Leah.

The friends all looked at each other, at a loss for what to do next. Well, all but Lalatco. Lalatco was, no doubt, the best tracker among them and it appeared to the others that he may have found something. Vurth was just about to ask him that very thing, but Elonda sensed Vurth's intention and motioned for him to be quiet. Vurth frowned at her but obliged. A few moments later, Lalatco motioned for Elonda to join him. As the two of them looked at an area and talked in quiet voices, Vurth's patience began to wane.

"Well, you two, we got something or not?" huffed the dwarf.

"I believe we do." After saying this, Lalatco reached up and found a handhold and started to climb a skinny spire. "But," he said as he climbed, "I need to get just a bit higher."

Elonda watched him for a moment, making sure that he looked comfortable, before turning her attention to the group. "Lalatco has found some very peculiar tracks. Small, maybe not even half the size of a track one of us would leave behind."

"Wolves?" asked Leah.

"No, for sure not wolves. They appear to be more human perhaps, but that does not seem right either." Elonda looked up again and saw Lalatco had reached the top of his climb and was surveying the area.

"So, if they are not wolves, why the interest?" Demorous asked as he spun his sword in his hand.

"Because," said Lalatco as he landed next to Elonda back on the path, "I can see some small huts not far from here, and I would bet that whoever calls those huts home can point us in the right direction."

The group followed Lalatco as they left the easier path and again enjoyed the frustration of traveling through the uneven terrain that was the spires. But it was not long before the group arrived at the huts. The huts were small, no taller than half the height of the taller Demorous. They were made out of rocks, not smooth stone like a castle, but with random-sized rocks fitting together in jagged patterns. Lalatco led the group into the small clearing where six huts stood.

"What do you want?" asked a squeaky voice from within one of the huts.

There was a moment of silence before anyone responded, not wanting to all speak at once. Jyres took the lead and answered. "We are searching for something and hoping you may be able to help us since you live here. We are not from here."

For a while all was silent. Then, one after another, small creatures exited the small homes. Two such creatures came out of each hut. The creatures were half the height of Vurth and had black fur. Their arms were long and skinny, and their tails were as long as they were tall. Large eyes lay under furry eyebrows and curved ears stuck out quite far from their heads.

The two creatures in front each carried a spear and walked right up to the group. "What are you searching for?" said that same squeaky voice. "How do we know it is safe to help you?"

"We are tracking dangerous wolves, who live somewhere near here." Jyres watched as the creatures looked at each other with wide eyes. "You know of these wolves?"

"Yes, we have to climb high above them when they come around so they cannot harm us."

"Can you show us where to find them?"

Simamar had kept his group moving as fast as possible, searching everywhere for any sign of the horde. That sign came a few days into the journey when they spotted the creature from a distance, to the east of Secord. Had it not been Simamar in the lead, who had a more aggressive nature, the group may not have been able to find the creature in the vast space that was the old world. But in the king's wisdom, he had chosen the right elf for the task.

Simamar and Karth made the plan together and Karth made sure it was communicated to the yixl. They hoped to surprise the horde and use the river to help lessen the possible escape routes for the creature. Using the cover of darkness, Simamar led the group along the small river toward the horde. The group was less than a rock's throw away before the horde spotted them. Then the race was on. The horde had no interest in finding out who was coming, his only interest was the gate. As he tried to back away and leave the area, Simamar's horse circled him forcing him back.

Before long the horde was encircled by the elves and yixl, and the river was at his back. The horde had enough of this. It charged Simamar. Simamar's horse reacted by prancing back, avoiding the horde for the moment. Simamar lashed out with his spear, catching the creature in its shoulder. The spear, with the specially made tip, penetrated the gelatinous body and the horde let out a muffled cry.

Simamar couldn't help but smile. The spears worked...and they were going to end this right now. His fellow elves on horseback, and the yixl on the ground, had the horde right where they wanted it. Simamar nodded, and the group started to close the circle tighter around the horde.

From out of the darkness came a guttural scream, followed by, "Click-Clack!" Bluey and his goblins came rushing towards the yixl with a fiery intensity. The yixl retreated from the sudden enemy, and as quick as Simamar had gained the advantage, he lost it in an instant. Simamar looked up to see Mit and another group of suspected enemies on their way to join the fight. As much as it pained him to admit it, he was outnumbered.

He called to the elves and they rushed in on their horses, pushing the goblins back for the moment. They wasted no time in pulling up the yixl to join them on the horses before thundering away from the goblins and the approaching reinforcements. Once they were a safe distance away, they slowed the horses to a trot.

Simamar cursed aloud. And Karth didn't bother to repeat it for the yixl. "We had it. The horde was ours!" Simamar cursed again and looked back toward the enemy, making sure they had not decided to pursue them. "And what was Mit doing with that rag-tag group, why would he interrupt us?"

"That is an excellent question," replied Karth. "But one I don't even have a guess for." Karth paused and then translated some of the conversation for the yixl. "At least the spear appeared to work," he said later as he gestured to the spear in Simamar's hand.

"There is that. But it brings me little consolation right now." Shaking his head Simamar turned back toward Mit and his band. "We are far too outnumbered, but part of me says we should organize an attack."

Karth translated to the yixl and Rutu responded right away. Karth nodded and turned to Simamar. "Rutu and I disagree. We have no chance in a fight. We must report this to the king as soon as possible, it is the only option."

Simamar, always one for aggression, conceded. "Very well, let us go with all speed."

Mit cursed to himself. Bluey was too impatient. He went headlong after those yixl as soon as he saw them. But no matter, the horde was here in front of him now. And that was what was needed.

"You are welcome," Mit announced to the creature.

The horde lifted his head in response but made no reply.

"I have heard a lot about you. And I am glad to see you in person."

"No more...time has...come." The horde started to walk in slow steady paces.

Mit turned to walk with him but left enough space between them to both so as not to crowd the horde and not become a target. "I only offer help."

"No more...no one helps."

"I don't need anything from you. I offer to escort you all the way to the gate. Our protection..." Mit gestured to all those around him. "...is yours. I hope that our saving you has at least granted us that much."

The horde looked confused for a moment before looking back at Mit. "Fine...walk...with."

As the group started to walk on, Mit surveyed the group with him. He had amassed quite a following. They had numbered 24 before they crossed the mountains and they had almost doubled that by the time they had finished crossing. Mit had done his work at Castle Mystic, but most of the credit for the rest went to Bluey. It was apparent that his name preceded him, for most of the orcs and goblins they crossed paths with on their way through the mountains chose to join the group based on Bluey's presence alone. An interesting match they were, Bluey and him. Both of them seemed to carry influence and desire, though the kind of influence and desire varied greatly.

Bluey came to walk with Mit, interrupting his thoughts. "Whatsss the plan now?"

Mit smiled. "Now, my over-eager friend, we get paid." This brought a large smile to the goblin's face and Mit smiled in return. He had known that answer would keep Bluey happy. But in truth, he had not worked everything out in his mind yet. He was not sure how long he would keep this group together as they were not a bunch that he placed great faith in when it came to loyalty. "Bluey," Mit questioned. "How long will these orcs and goblins follow you?"

Bluey considered the question for a moment. "Original goblinss, will follow. New oness, will follow long as see it helpss them. Long as we are winnings."

Mit thanked the goblin and walked on. He pushed the noises around him away as he considered how to ensure he kept the status quo.

26

Finding the Dire Wolves

The creatures talked in hushed voices as they discussed Jyres's question. After a few more moments the leader turned back to Jyres. "We need more information. Why do you want to find the wolves? And what does it have to do with us?"

"Good questions," Jyres replied. "We believe the wolves have something that does not belong to them. And as to the other question, we mean you no harm, but only ask for your help in directing us to them." Leah's eyes flicked to Jyres and then the others, looking to see if they shared the same nervousness she did as they awaited a response. But to their credit, they all maintained neutral faces and let Jyres continue the conversation. "We also understand that you want to keep your people safe."

The leader nodded, then turned back to the other creatures and their quiet conversation resumed. Jyres turned to the side, toward his group, and just shrugged. Lalatco patted his friend's shoulder as they returned their attention to these peculiar creatures. Their tails were always in motion, often curving up behind them. Jyres also noticed their ears twitch, often in sync with a tail movement. Interesting creatures and not like anything he had come across before.

The leader of the group came forward again. "The wolves are more aggressive now with the bigger wolves among them. We will help you. I think it will be a good thing for us."

"Excellent! And thank you." Letting his curiosity get the better of him, Jyres asked. "May I ask how it is that you can speak with us? I find it hard to believe you have seen many like us before."

Even with that simple question, the leader returned to his group to talk. This group of twelve creatures seemed to make every decision together. Jyres wondered how they got anything done. Did they even discuss everyday things in this way?

Turning back to Jyres, the leader said, "Long time now, a traveler passed through here and stayed with us a while. He taught us the language and we have used it every day since." The creature's tail bobbed up and down behind him as he spoke. "The visitor also gave us a name, smooqe. And that is what we call ourselves now."

Jyres smiled and nodded. Soon after, they began to plan and discuss what to do next. It was a painstakingly slow process, as the smooqe wanted to discuss everything as a group. Jyres tried very hard not to rush them, as he didn't want to do anything that would be an obstacle to the smooqe helping them find the wolves. After another arc had gone by, two smooqe were ready to lead Jyres and his friends to the wolves' lair. Jyres was pleasantly surprised that they also agreed to lead Gargan to the lair, as well, when night had fallen. It seemed that the smooqe were perhaps aware of gargoyles.

The two smooqe guides led the way, with Lalatco and Jyres close behind, and Elonda and Leah taking up the rear of the group. The path was not always easy and they all had to squeeze through some tight spots. The smooqe used their tails to their advantage, using them to help grasp or swing from things. Their hands and feet also appeared to be sticky or tacky for they had little problem hanging on the side of rocks or spires. Because of those attributes, the guides often found themselves waiting for their followers as they tried to climb over a spire or traverse uneven terrain.

Vurth seemed to be having the most difficult time with it, and to his chagrin, Demorous had to help him with some of the taller climbs. The fox, who continued to be Demorous's constant companion, handled the rocky ground well, and only used Demorous's shoulder as a way to continue on a few occasions. Lalatco and Elonda managed it well, their natural agility and slender frames helping them in ways that weren't possible for the others.

Nevertheless, as the day wore on, they grew closer to their destination. They came to a natural overlook that had a view of many of the lower spires. They rested there and even the smooqe guides seemed to relish the break. The group sat in silence, and Vurth even closed his eyes, taking the opportunity to rest. Then, sensing the group was ready, the smooqe explained why they had stopped at this spot. It provided an overview of the main path the wolves followed below. Going any further than this without being seen would be very difficult during the day. Lalatco and Jyres confirmed their understanding and agreed to take the first watch, allowing the others to continue resting.

It was not long before the elf spotted a wolf lumbering along a path below. Lalatco ducked behind the rocky wall and turned to make sure the others were out of sight. And they were. They were well back from the ledge and sitting against spires, not visible to wolves down below. Lalatco was quick to appreciate this spot the smooqe had chosen. It was easy for Lalatco to spy on the wolves below while staying hidden. The smooqe were right; it was a common path for the wolves and Lalatco tracked the movements of each wolf who passed by below.

As the arcs passed by the group took their turns at watch. While Vurth was on watch, Leah placed her quiver of arrows on the ground in front of her. She removed one arrow and pulled out some rope from her pack. With slow practiced motions, Leah secured one end of the rope to the arrow and then replaced the arrow in the quiver. Vurth turned to watch her as his curiosity increased. She removed another arrow from the quiver and pulled it close to inspect the fletching. Next, she pulled out a small clay jar from her pack. She scooped a small amount of the sticky substance from the jar and rubbed it across the shaft of the arrow.

Vurth's curiosity got the better of him. "So, um, what are you doing there lass?"

Leah looked up from her work with a smile. "Aren't you supposed to be looking that way?" she asked, pointing toward the paths below to emphasize the point.

Vurth shrugged. "Not much to look at, come on now, what are you up to?"

"It is always good to be prepared. Especially when you don't know exactly what you are up against." Leah finished putting the sticky goo on a second arrow and returned them to the quiver. "And it is a good way to spend some time as we wait."

"How do you know which arrow is which? There are a lot of arrows in that quiver of yours."

Leah gave him a half grin. "I know." She pulled one more arrow from the quiver and placed it on her lap. Looking up at the dwarf she said, "What do you think is going to happen, how is this going to end?"

Vurth turned back and surveyed the area he was supposed to be watching as he considered the question. "I have no idea," he said in a whisper. Turning back to Leah he said again, louder this time, "I just don't know. I wish I could tell you that I will be marching out of these forsaken spires with a trophy in my hand and confidence in what that meant. But.." his voice trailed off leaving the thought uncompleted.

"I am worried," she said as she used her knife to etch something into the shaft of the arrow. Vurth couldn't tell what it was from where he was keeping watch.

"I think we all are, lass." Vurth watched as Leah held up the arrow with her name etched into the wood. "Well done, but does it do anything special?"

"Only tells the one I hit who it was that caused it such pain," Leah said with a stone-straight face. And she held it for a moment before she started laughing.

Vurth chuckled at the human. "You had me worried there at first; thought too much of me had rubbed off on you."

"Vurth," she said, as she put the arrow away and walked over to him. "Too much of you would never be possible." She leaned down and planted a kiss on the cheek.

Vurth didn't know how to react, and a soft pink color appeared on his face. This only caused Leah to laugh as she returned to her husband, who was fast asleep.

As the day wore on and night approached, the number of wolf sightings decreased. The group assumed there were more and more of the wolves in the lair or headed to the lair the later it became, and as darkness fell, the wolves moving around below were few and far between. Gargan soon joined the group, a smooqe guiding him from his back as he glided. They then huddled together as the smooqe told them how far they still had to go to reach their destination.

With the plan set, the group left their guides on the ledge and made their way down to the main path that would lead them to the wolves and, they hoped, the Bear's Heart. Lalatco now became the guide, as he led the group along the path, making every attempt to remain as silent as possible. He held up his hand on a few occasions, stopping the group's progress. But each time they were able to continue soon after, as whatever Lalatco heard or saw moved on without incident.

A short time later, as the group was rounding a curve, Lalatco motioned everybody off the path and into the small spires adjacent to where they had been walking. Unsure of what forced Lalatco to do this, the group stayed quiet as Lalatco looked on from his spot. A few moments later the elf turned to the group. "All clear. Just down the way, there appears to be an entrance into a cave. I think it is safe to assume that it is the entrance to the wolves' lair."

"What are the chances of us walking in unnoticed?" asked Demorous.

Lalatco pondered that question before nodding his head just a bit to each side. "Hard to say. I think we will be able to make it to the entrance, but who knows what waits for us inside."

"Well, we don't have a lot of options," Elonda said with a determined voice. "We have no chance at all if we approach during the day. So it is either seeing how far we can go unnoticed or knocking on the door for a conversation with dire wolves."

"Then we see how far we can get. I have my doubts that we would be welcomed anyway."

The others nodded in agreement and turned to Lalatco, ready for him to lead them again. He took another look around the area, making sure no wolves had come near while they were talking, and stepped out from the spires and onto the path toward the cave. Lalatco traveled a little faster than the group had been moving, wanting to cover the distance to the cave as fast as possible while trying to maintain their silent approach. Before long the group was crowded around the entrance, half on each side of it.

The cave was dark and foreboding, offering little evidence of what may lay within. Jyres peered around the outer wall and into the darkness, but he couldn't make out a thing. Lalatco and Elonda fared better, but even their elven eyes were limited in the darkness. Gargan, who was used to the dark stepped forward to try and get a better look. He took a couple of more steps and entered the cave before kneeling and letting his eyes adjust to the lack of light around him. After a few long moments, he stepped back out, careful not to make more noise than necessary.

"There are two great wolves just inside the cave," he whispered to the others. "They didn't move at all, and I am thinking they are asleep."

Well, they had come this far. Lalatco led the way again as they entered the cave. He paused, much like Gargan had done, trying to establish where the wolves were in relation to the entrance. Lalatco put two fingers in the air, confirming what Gargan had told them, and then pointed in the direction of the sleeping wolves. Lalatco could also hear them now, their deep intake and exhale of breath standing out in an otherwise quiet cave. The elf started moving again, motioning for the others to follow. Every step was careful and calculated, evaluating every spot to place the next foot. The others tried to match the elf's silent movement, hoping to sneak past the wolves.

Gargan wasn't kidding. These two wolves were huge. By far the biggest wolves anyone in the group had ever seen. Their pure size heightened the tension in the air as they moved past them. One of Vurth's steps sent a small pebble rolling on the rocky floor and everyone stopped in their tracks as the tit-tat of the small pebble seemed so loud in this large noiseless space. For another moment no one moved, and everyone held their breath waiting for the two giant sleeping forms to react to the noise. But luck seemed to be on their side and, after nothing seemed to change in the wolves breathing, Lalatco moved the group on until they came to a tunnel that they would have to pass through. It was only wide enough for one person at a time, so they passed through to the other side in a single file.

As Lalatco led the group further into the dire wolves' lair, what little moonlight had filtered into the cave from the entrance was all but gone. As the darkness overwhelmed him, he called for a stop. "Gargan," Lalatco whispered, "your turn."

Gargan came forward to take the lead. His eyes, used to the dark, still struggled to make out much. After taking just a few steps Gargan looked back and realized no one moved with him. Thinking fast, he called to Jyres keeping his voice low. "Jyres, your rope." Jyres did as he was instructed, passing the rope up the line. As soon as Gargan had the rope, he tied one end around his wrist. He then passed the rope to Lalatco. "Have each person hold on to the rope behind me. As long as they hold on to the rope, I can guide them in this darkness."

Once that was done, Gargan began walking again. This time the others followed. With the darkness, the others could only see their hands in front of their face, and all else was black. Gargan could see a little better than that. But as he walked along, it was hard to make out much beyond the changes in the direction of the tunnels. Another step and then Gargan came to a halt. Out in front of him, he saw the whites of a pair of eyes like circles of color in the black. A wolf. Gargan didn't move, and the others, sensing something was amiss, didn't move or speak.

Unsure of his next action, Gargan waited. And waited, until the pair of eyes moved on. Gargan gave a small tug on the rope and the group began forward again. Then Gargan sensed a change in the tunnel rock to his left and realized he could continue straight or veer to the left. He went left. This continued for a while, stopping for wolves in the area, and turning down side passages. One such turn brought them to an abrupt dead end. And to Gargan's dismay, it also led to a wolf. The wolf was laying down in the passage, but very much awake.

Before the wolf could react, as it was even more surprised than the gargoyle, Gargan clamped a firm hand around the smaller wolf's snout. The wolf thrashed and clawed, but no sound was made, Gargan's tight grip forcing the wolf's mouth to stay closed. Lalatco came up alongside Gargan and thrust out with his scimitar, granting the wolf a quick death. Gargan released the dead wolf and the group doubled back on themselves to try a different tunnel and direction.

After another turn, Gargan still in the lead, they came across two sleeping wolves in their path. With the utmost care, he led the group, still all connected via the rope, around the sleeping creatures. And they walked on. After another turn, in the distance, the very hint of light started to penetrate the darkness. Gargan tugged on the rope and came to a stop. He tapped Lalatco. The elf stepped close to the gargoyle following his pointed finger. Lalatco could make out the form of a wolf walking at a slow pace away from them and toward the light. The wolf stopped walking and, pointing its snout in the air, began to sniff. With the soundless steps only a skilled elf can make, Lalatco snuck up on the wolf. With one thrust of his blade through the wolf's throat, he killed the wolf without making a sound.

The group continued toward the light. As they neared the end of the tunnel, it took an immediate right, which was where the light was coming from. The group let go of the rope and Gargan wound it up, returning it to Jyres's pack. Jyres, feeling unpleasant about having to kill the wolves without knowing full well what was going on, shook off the feelings. Taking a deep breath, he stayed as tight to the wall as possible and peered around the corner. The tunnel opened up to a very large cavern with multiple paths leading to it. Small holes in the rock high above let in moonlight, small beams of light casting the area in a dull gloomy glow. But what caught Jyres's attention was the mounds of rocks in the middle of the room where a large dire wolf lay. The wolf wore gold chains around his thick neck. Jyres scanned the rest of the room, and several wolves and a few bigger dire wolves were spread around the cavern. Jyres brought his head back around the corner and in a low voice explained what he saw to the group.

"No sign of anything that could be the Bear's Heart?" Leah asked.

Jyres shook his head and took another peek around the corner. His eyes roamed the area again, looking for anything that he might have missed. Nothing. Just as he was about to pull his head back, the wolf with the gold chain shifted, and there behind his massive frame was a wooden box. On top of the wooden box was an item. A moonbeam fell right over the item. Jyres's heart leaped in his chest. It was too far away to make out the details, but big enough for Jyres to see the shape of a bear in the middle of the item. He turned his attention back to his friends. With a big smile on his face, he said in a whisper, "I think we found it."

The group responded to Jyres words with silent cheers. "What are the chances we can get in and sneak off with it?" asked Lalatco.

Jyres shook his head, "very low, too many wolves." He then asked a question of his own. "Think we can talk our way out of it?"

Elonda was the one to respond this time. "We don't even know if they can communicate with us, and if they can, I don't think they are just going to let us take something from them."

"We can't just go in there and start killing wolves, that doesn't seem right." Jyres shook his head in frustration unsure of what to do next.

Sensing Jyres indecisiveness, Elonda said, "Let me take a look." She switched places with Jyres, her body tight to the wall, and peered around the tunnel. She took in the area, noting the things Jyres had already told them. She then counted the number of tunnels leading into and out of the big cave, seeing that one of them seemed to have more light than others. Turning back to the group she said, "I think we continue in as quietly as possible, shifting to the right as we enter, and make our way towards the item at the same time. We may not make it all the way to the Bear's Heart, but we will put ourselves in a better position."

No one knew of a better plan, and it made sense to those who hadn't yet seen the immense cavern they were about to enter. Elonda led the way this time, as the group filed out into the big space, following Elonda's path. She made her way at an angle that took them both towards the center pile of rocks and the tunnel that glowed brighter than the others. On their way, they stepped over sleeping wolves, knowing their luck was not going to hold. As if almost on queue, they heard a deep growl behind them, followed by one off to their left. Elonda forced herself, as did the rest of the group, to take a few more steps, getting her closer to her two targets.

Then a loud voice echoed throughout the chamber. It was a deep voice, the tone of which was amplified by the cavern. The dire wolf with the gold chains was now standing on the raised rocks. "We have intruders. How dare you enter our lair!" The wolves that were spread around the area all began to wake up and stand up, turning their attention to the trespassers.

The group came to a halt and Vurth could be heard saying, "Well, I guess they can talk."

Lalatco and Jyres stepped out in front. "We have been on a search," Jyres replied with more confidence than he was feeling. "This search led us here. We didn't know for sure who we would find at the end of our journey." Was it a stretch of the truth? Completely. But Jyres felt it was the safer answer.

"What search would bring you here? Leave us at once!" The large dire wolf took a step down to the next level of rock; still a couple more were left before he would be on the cave floor. The other wolves began a slow advance in the direction of the trespassers.

As the wolf was speaking, Jyres took the opportunity to focus his gaze on the item behind the dire wolf. It was about the size of a human head, a bit larger perhaps. The top of the item looked like a bear's head. Claws came down the side of it like the bear was holding onto what was in the middle. The middle was, in fact, a heart. It was a vibrant blue, with flames licking the edges. Jyres now did not doubt that he was, indeed, looking at the Bear's Heart. And since the dire wolves were talking, all their guesses about the item seemed to be proven correct.

"Please understand we mean no offense or harm, we are here to save the Kingdom of Calridian." Jyres rubbed the back of his hand across his forehead, suddenly feeling rather warm.

"Save the kingdom." The wolf laughed as he took another step down. "Do you take me as a fool?"

"No, actually, the exact opposite." Jyres took a deep breath and continued. "We have been in search of an item called the Bear's Heart. And unless my eyes deceive me, it does appear as though you are in possession of an item that would match that name."

"Jyres, what are you doing? Telling him everything?" questioned Demorous in a quiet voice.

Lalatco responded for him, "Look around. There are too many of them. This is our only chance."

The dire wolf glanced back at the item and growled. "This is ours. Its power grants us the ability to speak, and I am out of patience."

"Grant me just a moment longer," pleaded Jyres. "Although it may be in your possession, it does not belong to you. An enemy known as the horde will be unleashed on the world if we do not return to the Gate of Fire with the Bear's Heart. And because you are no fool, you know you will not be safe here. No one will be safe from the horde. We must stop them to keep everyone safe, including your wolves."

"This does not scare me, your gibberish is at an end. Last chance. Turn around and leave. Or die!"

Jyres's hopes were dashed in an instant. Any chance of working with the wolves was gone. On instinct, his hand dropped to his sword hilt at his side. But his mind stopped him from drawing the blade. He knew that if he drew his weapon he would force his friends to fight an almost impossible battle. One that may get them all killed. That was not a chance he was willing to take. But if he listened to the wolf and they turned around and left; would they all die anyway? Would the horde succeed at freeing the rest of his kind? How could he make a decision like this? He couldn't stand the thought of his friends dying in this cave because he decided to fight. They didn't even know if unmaking the spell would be helpful. Jyres shook his head and looked around the cave one more time, hoping beyond hope that some other option would present itself. But of course, nothing did.

The dire wolf started to smile. He was about to give the order. Jyres had to decide. He looked at the Bear's Heart behind the dire wolf one more time, what was the right answer?

Jyres turned his head just enough to look at Lalatco. Lalatco gave him a barely perceptible nod. Lalatco was Jyres's oldest friend. He was the one who started this crazy journey with him those years ago when they had searched for Zar. They knew each other well.

In that one small nod, Lalatco was telling him it was okay. They all understood. His friends knew what decision Jyres had to make. They were ready.

Jyres took a deep breath and pulled his sword from its sheath. Before his blade had even come clear, the leader of the wolves howled. And all the wolves in the cave charged.

28
The Battle for the Prize

The wolves attacked. The ferocity of the attack at first pushed the heroes back. Jyres took a few steps back as he used his sword to stop a wolf from tearing his neck open. Lalatco, with scimitars drawn, battled two wolves away, holding his ground. The others had all drawn their weapons as well, and Gargan used his natural strength to fight off the wolves nearest to him.

Vurth hacked at a wolf with his axe, catching it in its side and sending it to the ground. But he just got his axe up in time to stop a lunging wolf and its teeth. He took a step forward and used his shoulder to knock it off its feet. But when one wolf fell, two more were there to take its place. Vurth swung his axe in a wide arc keeping three wolves away from him.

Demorous, with his fox on his shoulder, used a combination of strength and steel to fight against the wolves. As one leaped at him he dodged to the left letting it go by him. Then he lashed out with a punch, connecting on the nearest wolf's face and breaking its jaw. At the same time, his sword in his other hand swiped to the side. It slashed a large wound into another wolf, leaving it all but dead on the ground. Demorous had clad himself in some of his armor for the trip, and he was glad for it. A wolf trying to claw him only succeeded in scratching up his shoulder plates.

Elonda and Leah, each with a sword, stood back to back, fending off the wolves who tried to breach their defenses. Few could, but this also meant little damage was done to the wolves. The battle continued like this for a while, the heroes scoring hits where they could, but often just ensuring they stayed alive.

"This isn't working," cried Vurth as he batted away another wolf.

Jyres couldn't agree more. "We must push forward, together." The group responded, increasing their attacks and taking steps in the direction of the center of the cave and the waiting prize. "Keep it up," Jyres urged his friends.

Just then, Leah was knocked to the ground. Two wolves leaped on top of her, teeth ready to tear her apart. But Gargan was there. He gripped each wolf with his bare hands and in one motion sent them flying away from Leah. Leah was quick to regain her feet before any other wolves could take advantage of the situation.

With each step, the group grew closer to their target. The dire wolf with the gold chains howled again. And a few wolves who had not joined the fight responded. They were dire wolves. Maybe not as big as their leader, but just as fierce. Two of the dire wolves charged at Jyres and Lalatco and all progress was halted. Jyres moved his sword as fast as he possibly could, but with each swing, he felt like he was getting closer and closer to not being fast enough. The wolves had claws, teeth, and strength. And they used them to what might ultimately prove to be deadly efficiency. Jyres heard a pained grunt from Vurth, but couldn't even think about looking to see if the dwarf was okay. His full attention was on defense against the powerful dire wolf in front of him.

Jyres jumped over a swipe of the wolf's claws and then scored a lucky cut on the wolf. It was not anything that was going to hamper the big wolf, but enough to buy him a moment. A quick look told him that they were all hard-pressed, and could not last at this pace. He cursed out loud and batted away another limb. Next to Jyres, Lalatco was having much the same result against the dire wolf in front of him. He had marked the wolf with a couple of cuts, but each hit had to be hard-earned.

They all sensed it. The tide had turned and they would soon be overwhelmed. Elonda however had other ideas. She jumped over one wolf and finished her jump by kicking another wolf out of the way. This was not going to be the end. She exploded towards the center rocks pouring all her energy into her speed. She spun away from the jaws of one wolf and ducked as another jumped at her.

Jyres realized what was happening and called to Elonda. "No! Elonda!" Jyres narrowly avoided what would have been a killing blow from the wolf as he focused on Elonda, the woman he loved, sprinting toward the large dire wolf and the Bear's Heart. Jyres screamed again, desperation in his voice, "Elonda!" So focused was he, that he hadn't heard Lalatco's orders, changing the defense. Gargan, who was to Jyres's right and behind him, pulled him back into the tight circle they had formed. Lalatco and Leah stood in the middle of the circle. Jyres, Gargan, Vurth, and Demorous stood little more than shoulder to shoulder from each other. Before Jyres had time to process what was happening, Lalatco and Leah started to fling knives and shoot arrows with unbelievable efficiency.

Lalatco and Leah trusted the others on the outside of the circle to do their job and concentrated all their attention on the area around Elonda. As Elonda ducked and weaved, knives and arrows struck home on wolves and dire wolves alike. Lalatco pulled another knife from his bandoleer and sent it with expert accuracy into the neck of a wolf just as Elonda approached it. Two wolves nipping at Elonda's heels were met with an arrow to the face as Leah started to go through her quiver with impressive speed. Jyres's hope soared as the skilled couple cleared the way for Elonda, who used every bit of speed and agility she possessed on her way to the raised rocks.

Jyres received a gash across his arm but sliced the wolf across its neck before it could strike again. Gargan and Demorous somehow seemed to increase their tenaciousness, helping to keep the archer and knife thrower safe from enemy attacks. Vurth had been bloodied, but his voice continued to spew out curses and battle lust as another wolf fell to his axe.

An arrow took care of the last wolf in Elonda's way and she leaped up to the first level of stone, the giant dire wolf now only one level above her. Time seemed to slow down as she spun and stepped to the side as the wolf snapped his jaws down at her. Using the momentum from her spin, Elonda jumped and spun her body again as she soared above the wolf. The wolf was lightning fast for its size and craned its neck locking its teeth onto its target.

Jyres watched with horror as he saw something lodged in between the wolf's teeth. And then he lost sight of Elonda, who completed the jump and landed behind the wolf. His eyes locked on the dire wolf as it reacted, turning its head, and a dark blue became visible, the color of Elonda's shirt, a contrast to the huge white teeth. A loud and piercing scream came from the wolf as the completely ripped sleeve fell from his mouth and he saw Elonda standing at the top of the rocks, the Bear's Heart in her hands.

Jyres cheered with unbridled joy and the wolves that were still fighting turned to see what their leader had screamed about. Elonda and the others wasted no time in taking advantage of the moment. Elonda jumped down the other side of the rocks, turned, and ran towards the tunnel she had seen earlier. Few wolves were there to oppose her due to the arrows and knives that had paved her way earlier. The rest of the group, understanding her intention, ran. Ran at full speed to meet her as the wolves regrouped.

Jyres and the others met Elonda at the entrance of the tunnel with cheers and smiles. They slowed as they entered the dim tunnel, unsure of what awaited them, but at least they were able to see a bit, as opposed to the way they had come. They were all smiles, despite some of the wounds they had received in the battle with the wolves. But the smiles were short-lived. Wolves came after them from everywhere now. Every tunnel they ran past brought more wolves into the chase.

They entered into another big cavern with moonlight pouring in through large gaps in the ceiling high above them. In front of them was a bridge of sorts, for the path narrowed and large chasms could be seen on both sides of the natural bridge. They ran on. It was wide enough for two of them at a time and they paired off as they ran across, with Gargan in the back of the pack. Just as they were about to reach the other side, a handful of wolves rushed out of the tunnel they were about to enter, stopping their progress. And wolves still rushed them from behind, making their position perilous at best.

Close-quarters fighting began. Jyres was exhausted and he felt like every swing of his sword would be his last. They had come this far. Somehow they had captured the Bear's Heart and somehow they had to figure out how to escape with it. But with each passing moment, it seemed more impossible. Half of them now stood on solid ground, while Elonda, Vurth, and Gargan remained a few steps away on the bridge. A wolf latched on to Gargan's arm, its teeth digging into hard skin. Gargan tried to shake it off, before using the wolf as a weapon and swinging it into another wolf, sending both of the beasts into the chasm. Gargan roared in pain as the teeth ripped holes into his arm before the wolf lost its hold.

Lalatco's scimitars were dancing again, flashing at the entrance to the tunnel, trying to stem the tide of oncoming wolves. One such wolf scored a hit on his hip, but he shook it off, stabbing it through its open mouth. Vurth received a gash across his upper arm, and it sent him to his knees. A wolf latched on to his foot but lost its hold as Gargan pulled Vurth back to his feet.

Jyres yelled as he stabbed his sword into yet another wolf. How many of them were there? "We are clear," he heard Lalatco call. But at that same moment, he saw a wolf clamp down on part of the Bear's Heart, still in Elonda's hand. The momentum of the wolf forced them to the right as Elonda held on tight to the Bear's Heart. Jyres didn't even have time to yell out a warning as wolf and elf went tumbling off the edge.

eah had seen it coming. Right as the beast grabbed hold of the Bear's Heart Leah locked eyes with Elonda. In one quick, smooth motion, Leah reached to the back of her quiver, grabbing the certain arrow that she knew was still there. She fired without hesitation as Elonda and the wolf started to topple over the edge. The arrow had a rope tied to it and the arrow flew towards the falling pair. The rope hooked on the back of her quiver started to uncoil at a rapid rate. "Demorous!" Leah yelled with urgency.

The arrow flew dangerously close to Elonda as she disappeared over the edge. Elonda's hand shot up and snatched the rope as it sped past her. At the same time, Demorous grabbed the end of the rope as it started to leave the back of the quiver. Demorous's superior strength was put to the test, as Elonda's full body weight swung on the other end of the rope. The wolf only held on to the Bear's Heart for a brief moment before it lost its grip and plunged into the darkness. Demorous held tight as Elonda's momentum sent her crashing against the chasm wall. Then, using her feet to brace herself, she began climbing up the rope.

The others held off the wolves coming after them over the bridge, and for the moment their path was clear. As soon as Elonda's feet reached the safety of the path, they were off, running down the path as the light started to decrease the farther away they got from the bridge. *But it didn't matter*, Jyres thought. They were going to do this. They were going to make it. Against all odds, they were all still together.

The darkness threatened to take over again, but Leah grabbed an arrow, another speical one she had prepared, and with a flick of a rock against its shaft, it lit up with fire. She fired it and it smacked into a far opposite wall, granting them light for a time. Lalatco, still in the lead, led them through the tunnel, past the fire arrow, and down another passage. The light from the fire dimmed as they followed that passage and put the arrow behind them. But as the light from the fire dimmed, moonlight reached them again.

Jyres recognized where they were. The tunnel that was small and narrow was coming up next. That tunnel led to the cavern's exit and their freedom. But before he could even process that in his mind, and savor the thrill it would have brought, Jyres saw two huge dire wolves, standing right next to that narrow tunnel. They had to be the two dire wolves that had been sleeping in the entryway. They had come inside the cave and now stood between the heroes and their exit.

Lalatco paused, unsure of how to get by these massive creatures. The creatures growled and crouched, their intentions clear. As the group hesitated, Vurth exploded forward, charging right at one of the dire wolves. The large creature was at least three times the size of the dwarf, and it was more than evident that Vurth was overmatched. But Vurth thought otherwise. He ducked under the creature's head as it snapped at him. Vurth then sliced it across its leg, causing it to back up and put his weight on the back legs.

Gargan, seeing an opportunity, ran at the other dire wolf, who stood at least as tall as the gargoyle. He dodged one swipe of a paw from the beast and threw all his body weight into the wolf. The wolf gave ground by the smallest of margins. But it was enough. Lalatco, Leah, and Elonda all broke for the small tunnel. Jyres was right behind them, watching as the three slender figures slipped between the fighting and into the tunnel. As Jyres reached the tunnel with Demorous right alongside, he yelled to Vurth. "Time to go!"

Vurth had just finished striking the wolf in the side with his axe, the axe sinking into the wolf's flesh. The wolf howled and craned its neck to snap at the dwarf's leg. Vurth pulled at the axe to move aside, but the axe was in deep and it slowed his movement. Vurth let out a deep yell as the wolf's mouth closed around his leg.

Jyres and Demorous looked on in horror. There hung Vurth, his leg in the mouth of the wolf. Vurth screamed in pain as the wolf bit down harder, crushing bone.

"Vurth," Jyres yelled as he and Demorous moved to assist. Demorous brushed off a swipe of a paw from the wolf and jumped with his sword swinging, catching the wolf in the chest. The wolf swiped again, this time knocking the former knight to the ground. His trusty fox jumped from her curled spot around Demorous's neck and onto the wolf's face. The fox raked her paw across one of the wolf's eyes. In response, the wolf threw the prize hanging from his mouth and Vurth hit the wall with a sickening smack. The fox lost its footing with the sudden motion and fell. Before the fox hit the ground the dire wolf closed his mouth around the falling creature. And Mezzo was no more. Jyres slid past the side of the wolf, striking it across its already injured leg. The huge wolf collapsed on the useless leg. Demorous, enraged from witnessing the punishment on his friend and fox, let out a battle cry and jumped on top of the creature. The wolf shook his head trying to dislodge Demorous. But Demorous was going to take his revenge and he plunged his sword straight down through the beast's neck.

Jyres ran to his friend and knelt by him. "Vurth!" he screamed. "Vurth, stay with me!" Jyres got no response. He scanned the dwarf's body and Jyres's heart dropped. His dear friend had cuts, bruises, blood, and exposed bone. With absolute dread, he felt for a pulse, and there was nothing there. Vurth, Son of Rand, was dead. Jyres screamed; a sound of absolute agony.

Meanwhile, Gargan had had his hands full with the other wolf. He was trading blows and holding the wolf off. Then he heard Jyres's scream and heard the howls of many more wolves. He looked to see wolves coming from every tunnel and every corner of the caverns. Gargan pushed the dire wolf away, ducked under its jaws, and sent an uppercut right under its head, the wolf's head snapped back and the wolf went down in a heap. With no time to spare Gargan turned to see Demorous scooping up Vurth and urging Jyres on. Gargan scooped up Jyres and slung him over one shoulder, his friend lost to grief.

Demorous handed the lifeless body of Vurth to Gargan's other arm and the knight strapped Vurth's axe to the dwarf's belt. "Go," he said as he turned to face the oncoming wave.

Gargan was frozen in his spot for a moment. "Come on," he yelled to the knight.

"You need more time," said Demorous. He looked toward the big gargoyle one last time. "His sacrifice will not be for nothing." As Gargan started to move into the narrow tunnel. Demorous stepped just inside as the sounds of wolves came closer and closer. "Now go!" Demorous screamed. He flipped the hilt of his sword in his hand once before readying the blade in front of him. Through him was the only way to attack the rest of his new friends. But the wolves would never reach them. Not while he still breathed.

Gargan moved as fast as he could through the tight tunnel. A space that was even smaller when carrying two people. He exited the tunnel and came into the entry cavern. He saw Lalatco, Leah, and Elonda finishing their run to the exit. He heard an intense scream behind him, and he turned one last time to see Demorous standing like an immovable wall in the face of an unstoppable force. Gargan heard a grunt of pain and knew the time was short.

With a wordless thank you to the former night who had once been an enemy, Gargan turned and ran.

As he ran Gargan watched Leah pull an arrow from her quiver and a moment later the arrow was on fire. As Gargan arrived she let it fly through the air. A beacon of flame in a dark night filled with sorrow. Leah, Elonda, and Lalatco all fell speechless as they beheld what had happened to their friend Vurth. Tears came fast to the girls' eyes. But Lalatco's warrior training kicked in, pushing the pain aside. There would be time to mourn. Right now was not that time.

"Where is Demorous?" Lalatco asked Gargan.

"Buying us time," came the somber response. Gargan set Jyres on the ground, who had composed himself somewhat.

Lalatco breathed in deep. He looked over his group of friends. Every one of them had sustained injuries. Cuts here, blood there. Elonda still clutched the Bear's Heart in her hand, but they were exhausted, their energy spent. Lalatco nodded to the group. "Gargan's clan will have seen the flame. We get some distance from this place and we will be safe. Run with me, with everything you have left."

They ran into the night.

As a mighty warrior struck down yet another wolf, he yelled in triumph. A pair of wolves attacked from the side, knocking him to the ground. He smiled, there were worse ways to go. The fangs of a wolf found the warrior's neck...and the brave knight breathed his last.

In the very late arcs of the night, King Malick, Tagro, and many others arrived at the Gate of Fire. As they were growing close to the gate, they were joined by a scout returning from his mission. The scout reported to the king that his nephew, Simamar, was waiting for them along with Karth and the yixl at the gate. The king dismissed the scout and the large group of warriors started moving again.

Shepherd Rowland, on horseback, riding right next to the king, leaned over. "Is that good news, or bad news?"

"I am not sure, Shepherd. I was wondering the same thing. Either they were successful or have some not-so-good news. Whichever it is, we need to get there quickly, the night is almost over."

The group went as fast as a group their size could travel and Simamar was brought before the king as soon as they arrived.

"Report," said the king, with nervous anticipation as to what the report would be.

The young elf took a deep breath. "We were able to find the horde..." after a pause, "We had it." The elf's frustration boiled over again, they had been so close. "We had encircled the horde. He tried to escape but the spears worked. Sire, they worked."

"I see. But?" The king sensed bad news was on the way.

"Mit showed up, and ruined everything." Simamar shook his head, his intense disappointment was evident.

"Mit!" exclaimed Malick. "That does not make any sense." Of all the things he and Lord Kapel had discussed and painstakingly planned for, interference from Mit was not one of them.

"He had a small army with him, and there were too many of them for our small group. I am sorry, Uncle." Simamar bowed his head. The nephew was always looking for ways to please the uncle. And in this, perhaps the most important task imaginable, he had failed.

Malick pushed away the frustration and confusion for the moment. "Head up, nephew. You were not prepared to take on a large force. And you have confirmed that our spears work. Hope is not lost."

Simamar bowed one more time and turned away, leaving the king to attend to his many needed duties.

"Lord Kapel," Malick shouted over the noise of the army behind him. Once the lord had arrived at the king's side, he continued in a softer voice. "We are losing the dark, and soon the sun will be upon us. Make sure the gargoyle Hawkins is in position, we do not know when or if we will need to do the spell."

"Right away." Kapel also bowed and then moved through the men, dwarves, and elves to find the few gargoyles in the group.

Malick paused a moment. He looked across the open terrain to see the ring of fire and the gate. They both burned bright in the night. What would the next day bring? What would happen if the spell had to be performed? And why in the name of all things good is Mit leading an army? He shook his head as Tagro, son of Vurth, approached, and Malick's moment to think was gone as fast as it had come.

"Sire, the army is well, all things are ready. What are your orders?

"I don't know," he said aloud.

This took Tagro by surprise, as the king had always presented a confident front, a decisive decision-maker. Unsure of what to say next, Tagro started by saying, "Um, of course, we will stand ready."

"I apologize Tagro, son of Vurth. Let's move closer to the ring. In light of the information from Simamar, we need to be ready. Once we have moved, yes, have the army ready. Do whatever is needed to keep them fresh and alert. Assign some of the soldiers to set up the command tent. Then we wait."

Tagro bowed before heading back to the waiting lines of soldiers. As Tagro left and the orders were spread, the king found himself searching the crowd. Not for anyone in particular, but looking over the brave souls from the Kingdom of Calridian. Whatever happened in the coming arcs or days, this kingdom would continue. He would make sure of that. As he observed the group and they began to move again, four distinct shapes appeared in the distance. The dragons. The dragons had stayed at the castle a little longer, giving Cyna and Lumpkin as much time as possible to practice the words of the spell. The dragons of course were able to travel the distance in a lot less time.

Sometime later, Lord Kapel found the king again. "Hawkins is in place."

"Excellent. And the dragons have arrived."

"And...look to the west. The sky is full of gargoyles."

The king turned his head to look in the direction Lord Kapel had indicated. And he was right. Gargoyles did seem to be flooding the skies to the west. Something was happening; probably something of great importance.

Shepherd, still nearby, took a few steps closer to his fellow Council of Peace members. "That can't be good," he said, gesturing towards the gargoyles.

Lord Kapel smiled. "Well, perhaps not, or perhaps it is just what we need. Something tells me we will indeed find out soon."

The three of them looked on as the army moved and flowed around them, preparing to set up as close as possible to the eastern side of the ring of fire. They all let the silence linger, each lost to their own thoughts. Memories of Meslar and the events leading up to his demise flowed through Lord Kapel's mind. It was only a few years ago that the battle with Meslar and Bram took place, not far from where they stood. Signs were now starting to point to another battle being fought in the shadows of the gate. After a while, the three members nodded to each other and joined the army as it walked.

Tagro worked to organize the soldiers and rotate those on watch and those on rest. Those assigned to raise the small tent had almost completed their task as the dragons landed nearby. Cyna and Lumpkin were both astride Crimson, and they took care as they made their way to the ground. As soon as the tent was up, King Malick, Lord Kapel, Tagro, Simamar, and Shepherd put it to use. One flap was left open, and Esmerlada came and lay down, orientating herself so she could see in the tent and at the same time prevent others from entering. The king looked around the circle and then updated Esmerlada on what Simamar had reported earlier.

"It is safe to assume that Mit and the hoard will be here soon," said Simamar. "We would not have beaten them here by more than a day."

"Agreed," replied the king. "We must plan to defend against his small army. Tagro, thoughts?"

"We will have the numbers on them," the dwarf replied. "But they could come at the gate from any direction. If we thin out our numbers all the way around the gate, they could attack one area."

Lord Kapel nodded. "Not from any direction. They cannot approach from the south due to our position and the spires. I know you had traveled a few years ago with the dwarves through the tunnels under the spires to the north, but I find it hard to imagine Mit doing the same. We must plan for what would be the most logical. And from what we know from Simamar's confrontation with them, the most logical would be to come to the eastern side of the gate, where we now stand. But it would be possible to come from the west if they traveled around the northern dark mountains."

"It would take more time to take that route," replied Simamar, "an extra day at the least."

Malick thought that through for a moment. What would be most logical? "The problem is that we do not know what Mit's end game is. Which makes it hard to predict his actions. We also need to be ready for the spell, in case something goes wrong."

Esmeralda, who had been following the conversation closely, was the next to speak. "We must split the force in two. Guard both sides of the gate. We have the strength to do that."

"Aye, we could handle two sides," agreed Tagro.

"Very well, Tagro, make the arrangements. Lord Kapel, what do you need to make certain that those assigned can reach their places around the ring of fire?"

"Just a few others to go with me, and we will mark out the exact spots needed. Once ordered, all they will need is time to get to their spot." Before setting off, Lord Kapel added, "It should be mentioned that the Wanderer has not arrived yet with the black donosin."

"Good, make it happen," Malick nodded. "I know. Neither has Jyres arrived with the Bear's Heart. The next thing to do is to scout the area. So we know when Mit is drawing near or if anyone else approaches. Finally, let's see what is happening on the western side of the gate and where all the gargoyles are headed. Perhaps it will shed some light on our situation. Esmeralda, as soon as you and the other dragons are ready, begin flying over that area and see what you can learn."

As the group talked, the sun rose, and the ring and the gate burned on. Their never-ending flames were somehow even more disturbing during the magic that was a sunrise.

Just as Lalatco had instructed, the group ran out into the night. They charged down the path they had watched the wolves travel earlier that night. They ran as fast as they dared on the rocky terrain. Before long the rocky path was no longer obvious and they had to slow their escape. And soon they thought they were lost. But by either a stroke of good fortune or through a planned happening by the smooqe, two of the helpful creatures appeared. They led the way out of the spires and onto the plain on the western side of the Gate of Fire. Then the creatures were gone, just as fast as they had arrived.

The group paused, exhausted, in mourning, and beyond spent. Through it all, however, they had claimed the Bear's Heart. Then as if the wolves could hear their thoughts, howls echoed into the night as wolves emerged from the dark spires. The group looked at each other and then fell to their knees, they didn't have the strength to continue. The wolves started to approach them, and they all formed a tight circle, hugging each other close. Tears began to well in everyone's eyes.

"Take heart," Gargan's voice was like a thunderclap in the quiet night. "We are not alone."

They pulled their eyes from each other and looked to the skies. Gargoyles! Gargoyles were here! Dozens of them dropped from the sky and formed a protective circle around the heroes. And not for the first time, Jyres thanked the stars for meeting Gargan those short years ago. His kind was saving them again. More and more gargoyles arrived, doubling the circle of protection. The wolves, seeing this, retreated in frustration. They would not catch the intruders this night.

Jyres grabbed Elonda, holding her tight. Leah and Lalatco did much the same. They had pulled through. But not all of them. Gargan, still holding the body of Vurth, lowered him to the ground with care. The four remaining friends knelt around him. There was no stopping the tears now. They all cried for their dear friend, whom they would all miss. Lalatco grabbed Leah's hand, who in turn placed her hand in Elonda's. Once all four of them were holding hands, Lalatco started to sing. It was the same song Elonda and he had sung around the campfire. But this time they sang it to Vurth. As they ended with the final lines, "My friendship has been and is always here; Distance has no meaning here," their sadness, though still present, gave way to the love they had for him and each other.

Gargan knelt now, took the axe from the dwarf's belt, and placed it on Vurth's chest. He moved the dwarf's hands to encircle the handle. "I do not know if will be able to help in the coming battle, the sun comes to greet us. Let me do one last thing for my friend Vurth."

The others backed up a little, allowing the big gargoyle more space. Although Jyres was unsure of what Gargan was going to do, he never doubted his intentions and put his full faith in the gargoyle. Gargan placed his hands on the dwarf's shoulders. As the sun started to bathe the land with its light, Jyres and the others looked on in amazement. Vurth, laid out in perfect position started to turn into stone.

Gargan released his hands and turned to Jyres. "Now we will never forget him, his features, or his friendship." Gargan smiled, perhaps the biggest smile Jyres had ever seen on the big gargoyle. Then he too turned to stone.

Jyres crawled over to Vurth's body turned to a statue and reached a hand to his face. "Thank you," was all he could say.

The dragons rested their wings but promised the king that they would scout the area soon. A short while later, as the day moon moved in its pattern, marking the second arc of the day, the dragons began their search of the area. Esmeralda and Crimson took turns flying over the nearby regions staying on the lookout for anyone approaching. Esmeralda flew over the stone gargoyles on the western side of the gate, noting their defensive position. But Lalatco, Elonda, Jyres, and Leah went undetected among the stone statues. The group of four, needing to regain their energy, had fallen asleep right after the gargoyles had turned to stone.

As the dragons began their flight, Tagro and half of the army started their trek around the ring of fire toward the western side of the gate. This left the king and half the army behind to guard the eastern side. Lord Kapel kept busy. He brought Sigmon, Digmon, and Felix with him and they began to plot out and mark the required spots for the Ring of the Seventeen. This was a slow process, Lord Kapel taking care not to make any mistakes on the exact positions needed for the Seventeen.

Tagro and half the army had completed their move and not long after Lord Kapel had finished his marking. Crimson landed near Tagro's army with a roar, signaling to others that something was amiss. Mit and his group of bandits had been spotted.

On the other side of the ring of fire, which encircled the gate, Esmeralda was reporting much the same thing to the king. Mit was indeed approaching the gate via the most anticipated route, the eastern side. With the army split, the king was still feeling comfortable with the number of soldiers he had and ordered Tagro to stay where he was and to be ready for the signal. Another arc went by before Mit and his group came into view.

"Orders, Sire?" asked an elf that had been left in charge of soldiers with the king.

"We will let them come to us...patience."

A short time later, Mit and his band of misfits stopped their approach, just out of bow range from the king's army. Mit turned to the hoard who had walked with them the whole way. "As we talked about, I offer you my protection. I see many spears in that army ahead of us. I will go and talk with them, stay here, and you will be protected from the spears." Mit started to walk away from the hoard and Bluey followed. In a hushed voice, he said to the goblin, "Watch the creature, I will go talk with the king and come back with something of much more value."

The goblin nodded. Not in agreement, but because that was what Mit was expecting him to do. Bluey didn't understand what Mit was going to do Once Mit started walking away from him, with two others as support, Bluey went to stand by the hoard as he observed Mit. Mit and two others they had recruited at Castle Mystic continued to walk toward the king's army. They stopped about halfway there, waiting for the king or his spokesperson to meet them.

King Malick watched with curiosity as Mit left the main force and stopped, an obvious invitation for discussion. They had also spotted the horde in the group, and this made Malick wonder how the hoard would benefit from being swith Mit and his group. The king would go out to meet Mit, if nothing else, to try and learn what game Mit was playing. But the horde was here now, and the key was either with the group or the horde. This Malick did not like in the slightest. King Malick, Simamar, and Shepherd Rowland went out on horseback to meet Mit Merrituk.

As they trotted toward the former ambassador, Shepherd said, "No sudden movements but look to your left."

The king made an effort to look casual as he shifted his gaze to his left and the north. Three black donosin were lumbering away from the mountains and toward the ring of fire. This was a good thing, indeed. But he wondered why the Wanderer was not with them. The king returned his attention to the task at hand as they approached Mit and his accomplices.

"Hello, King," said Mit. "Nice to see you again," he said in a tone that didn't match the message.

"What is this?" asked Malcik, gesturing to the group behind Mit.

"No small talk? Very well. Let's get right to it, shall we?" smiled Mit. "As you can see, the horde is with me now."

"I see the horde. But I don't understand what you stand to gain in all this. The horde is dangerous."

Mit laughed. "King Malick, so sure you were that you could create a kingdom where everyone has peace and we are all one together. I helped you do that, but what did I get in return? Nothing. And the horde? Dangerous you say? It hasn't threatened me at all."

"As soon as you do anything besides help it open the gate, it will kill you. Have you seen the Silver Shadow? I don't think it is hard to imagine what happened to him. The horde, once loose, will trample the kingdom and all creatures who live in it."

"I see. So you would do anything to prevent that from happening correct?"

Malick didn't like the sound of that. And he knew Mit had something swirling around in that scheming brain of his. But he did not anticipate the human's next words.

"Name me the heir to the throne, and you can have the horde." Mit smiled wide as if he could already see himself as the King of Calridian.

King Malick, looking down on Mit from his mounted position, didn't know how to respond. Heir to the throne? Why? Malick would live longer than Mit, it made no sense. Mit must have sensed the king's confusion, because he spoke again before the king had made any response.

"I know what you're thinking, that you could be king forever with your elven gift of immortality. But was it not your father who had died long before he was supposed to? And how many elves died in the battles with Meslar? And even if I never become king, there is nothing wrong with being the second most powerful person in the kingdom, now is there?"

Malick looked to his nephew, who was perhaps the heir to the throne, though it had never been made official. The elf's eyes were dark and threatening, staring back at the former ambassador. Shepherd Rowland, kept his feelings hidden, not voicing his opinions or reacting to the statements. As the king thought it through, he didn't think for even a moment that Mit would be happy with second in command. He would be looking for ways to take the last step until he ascended to the throne.

After a few arcs of rest, Jyres, Leah, Lalatco, and Elonda stretched and began to move around. They knew there would be much more to do. Jyres looked around the circle of their stone protectors, appreciating them again before he turned his vision toward the Gate of Fire. They were not that far from it now. The ring and gate were in between the two dark mountain ranges, and their exit point had led them out onto the terrain on the western side of the gate. As Jyres looked toward the ring of fire, he called out to his friends. "I think I see some movement."

Lalatco climbed up to stand on top of one of the stone gargoyles to get a better view. As he focused on the direction Jyres had been facing, his elven eyes were indeed able to pick out an army near the ring of fire. "You are right, my friend," said Lalatco. "An army from Calridian has taken up position outside the ring of fire."

Elonda looked toward Lalatco. "That could mean the Bear's Heart will be needed soon," she said as she tapped on the item attached to her belt.

"It could mean a lot of things," said Leah. "Only one way to find out."

All four of them started out, their faces a mask of grim determination as the headed toward their fellow Calridians.

As the king and Mit talked, Bluey looked on. He didn't like what was taking so long. And he didn't like that Mit had left him here and didn't bring him along. He looked to the horde, whose eyes were fixed on the gate. "I will takes the key there," said Bluey.

The horde looked at him in surprise and then looked at the key held in its hand. "It...is...time."

Bluey walked over to the few horses that were with the group. He grabbed the reins of two horses and led them to the horde. Bluey was not graceful when it came to animals, but he managed to get into the saddle. The horde, copying the movements of the goblin, placed itself on the second horse, careful to only touch the saddle. Together they thundered away from the group. Shouts of alarm went up from the army of bandits. But none were fast enough to react. Bluey, the horde, and the key were on their way to the gate.

Malick stared back at Mit. If Mit could turn the horde over to him, it was something he had to consider. It would mean the gate would not be open, for they had the spears to keep this one horde away from the gate. And they could regain the key. But before the king could give it full consideration, a shout went up from Mit's assembled bandits. On horseback, a goblin and the horde thundered toward the ring of fire. Heading in a parallel direction to the king's army.

"What is this?" Simamar cried at Mit.

Mit turned to see what Simamar was talking about and a look of pure shock crossed his face, followed by one of uncertainty. "This was not what was planned," Mit stammered.

The king had seen the emotions cross his face and knew Mit was telling the truth. "Go," Malick yelled to his nephew.

But as Simamar pressed his heels to the horse, one of the men with Mit removed a knife from his belt and flung it at the horse. The knife hit the horse in the chest and the horse bucked back hard, causing Simamar to lose his grip. Mit retreated in panic, as Simamar's horse fell to the ground. The king looked back toward his army and raised his sword high. He then dropped it in one quick motion and a moment later arrows darkened in the sky, on their way toward the two horses and their riders as they thundered toward the gate. Simamar rolled to his feet and was quick to spring to the back of Shepherd's horse. The two of them, along with the king, raced back toward their army.

Bluey urged his horse on as they pressed toward the ring. Bluey was leading the horde to the northern part of the ring, trying to keep space between their horses and the Calridian army. Arrows began to fall around them, though they did not find their mark, and the space in between was increasing, causing the shot to become even more difficult for the archers. Bluey smiled, no one could kill Bluey.

King Malick rode into camp and looked back over his shoulder to see the goblin, horde, and horses ride free of the falling arrows, growing closer to their destination. Malick searched the area until he found the one he was looking for, a big dwarf, with a long trumpet tucked under his arm.

"One blast!" the king yelled.

The dwarf responded. Setting his lips to the trumpet and blowing out one long and thunderous note; a prearranged signal to the army. The king nodded to him. One way or another, things were about to change.

Jyres, Elonda, Lalatco, and Leah arrived at Tagro's position just as a trumpet sounded, filling the area with sound. Tagro began barking out orders in quick succession before running up to the four weary travelers. Tagro's face turned from hope to panic in a flash. "Father? Where is he?"

Leah responded for the group. "He didn't make it," she said with compassion. "But we wouldn't have captured the Bear's Heart without him."

Tagro, son of Vurth, dropped to one knee. In a quiet voice, he managed to say, "How?"

More chaos rose up around them and they all turned to see wolves. Wolves and dire wolves coming this way.

"That's how," Elonda said.

The young dwarf stood up, holding his axe tight, with steel in his voice he said, "Then let them come."

After a moment, Jyres moved to stand next to the dwarf, putting his hand on Tagro's shoulder. "What is going on here, why the horn blast?"

"It is the first signal, calling all of the Seventeen to their posts. The next signal will call for the start of the spell."

"But they don't even know that we had the Bear's Heart," said Elonda, holding the mystical item in her hands.

"Aye, we will send word. Crimson flies fast.

"Where do you need us?" asked Jyres.

Tagro thought about that for a moment. "If you were a dwarf I would send you to my spot on the ring so I could stay and send these wolves to their graves. But we also need to make sure that the Bear's Heart stays in place. See that spot marked there," continued Tagro. "That's where the Bear's Heart goes."

Lalatco stepped forward. "Leah and I are not done yet. We will take command for you. Go to your post. We will deal retribution."

Tagro grasped his hand and with steel in his voice said, "See that you do." With that, Tagro nodded and headed toward his spot around the ring.

Lalatco's and Jyres's eyes met and Lalatco pulled him in for a hug. "Go! Protect Cyna. We will fend off the mighty wolves."

Jyres stepped back and reached for Elonda's hand as Leah came up to grab Lalatco's. "We will see each other again," she said. "I know it."

Elonda smiling, but not one of true happiness because of the need to leave their friends, handed Leah the Bear's Heart. "It is yours now."

Grabbing ahold of the item Leah said, "It won't be moved from its needed place in the ring. I guarantee it. Now go protect our wizard."

Fighting back tears, Elonda and Jyres broke away from their dear friends and, finding Crimson, climbed on the dragon before he left for the other side of the gate. Elonda and Jyres looked down upon the area as Crimson sped to the other side. The two armies of Calridian began to get thinner and thinner as those who were part of the Seventeen and those assigned to protect them raced to surround the entire ring of fire. If only it was night, the gargoyles would double the size of their army. Jyres spied a lone horse standing just outside the ring of fire and a feeling of terror rose in his gut. Was it too late?

Crimson landed with a rush, as others around him continued their movement to the assigned positions. Elonda and Jyres climbed down from the dragon's back, and Crimson was gone as fast as he had come, going to take his position around the ring, nearest to the Bear's Heart. Elonda, on seeing the king, yelled out to him, forgetting his title in her urgency. "Malick," she called. "We are here."

Malick ran up to the two warriors. "Good to see you both." Then with intensity in his voice, he said, "Do you have it? The Bear's Heart?"

Jyres nodded. "We found it. Lalatco and Leah are putting it in place now." After a pause, Jyres bowed his head. "Vurth and Demorous didn't make it."

Malick knew he didn't have time for questions. "Well done. We now have a chance. Let's make sure their loss is not in vain. The horde and the key will be at the edge of the fire by now." The king shook his head. "We need to get in position. On three short horn blasts, the spell will start. Remember, it needs to be said three times."

"I understand," said Jyres. "Good luck, Sire."

"Good luck to all of us." The king clasped them both on the shoulders before heading off to his space around the ring of fire.

Elonda and Jyres ran toward Esmeralda, for they knew Cyna would be close. "Cyna," Jyres called as soon as they were within ear shot. Cyna turned and her face lit up with delight in seeing her brother and Elonda. The three of them encircled each other in a big hug.

"You're here!" Cyna said.

"We are. We found the Bear's Heart," sighed Jyres. "But this is not over yet. I told you I would be here with you, Cyna. At the end. I am sorry it has come to this."

Cyna blew out a long breath. She was shaking, the nervousness of the situation overwhelming the 12-year-old girl. "I know the spell," she said. "I just don't know how they think I have the power to do this."

"You can do this Cyna," said Elonda. "No one will be allowed to interrupt you, we will make sure of it."

Bluey and the horde dismounted from the horses. They looked to their left and right and saw soldiers, starting to come in their direction. The horde, with the key in hand, took its first step into the fire, and then a second. There it seemed to hesitate, as if it didn't know where it was. Bluey seeing this, and knowing nothing about the prophesy and needing to have no fear, stepped into the fire beside the horde. The horde took another step, as did Bluey.

Again, the horde hesitated. Bluey was not a patient goblin. He tore the key from the horde's hand. It came free with ease as the horde struggled with whatever was slowing it down.

Bluey looked to the gate, not far from them now. No fears assaulted him. No thoughts slowed him. Because nothing had ever been able to kill Bluey. He had nothing to fear, not even death itself. Bluey raced on toward the gate, neither stopping nor slowing. Upon reaching the gate, he smiled, pondering what secrets this gate could hold. Reaching the shield-shaped key to the gate, he fitted it into the slot. As soon as he did, the mystical gate began to open. Bluey's eyes filled with wonder as he took in his first peek into another world. There was the horde. A vast number of the creatures stood before him. They had been trapped forever in this mystical prison. Now, the gate was open.

The horde rushed forward in unison, flooding out of the gate in waves. The horde left the gate in all directions. But many surged right towards Bluey, who had no time to react. They rushed over him and through him like he was nothing. Because that's what he was to the hoard. Nothing. Bluey felt screams inside him as the bodies of the horde washed over him. Why? What was happening? Bluey gasped in pain as horde hands shoved him one way and the other. And then, Bluey, the goblin who had seemingly had an unlimited amount of luck, screamed in denial one last time...and died.

The horde started to fill the space between the ring of fire and the gate. The one horde who had escaped was no longer alone. He felt the emotion coming from the mob. They all felt it, together. First, freedom. Then, as they looked around and saw dwarves, dragons, elves, bears, and more circling the ring of fire, they all felt something else. Revenge. For this was the same situation that they had seen when they had been cast into the gate all those years ago. All the races were on the outside of the ring when they were on the inside. They had no idea how many years it had been. They had no recollection of who had first sentenced them to their fate. All they saw were the same races, the same ring of people. This time, they, the horde would not be imprisoned. They would win. Together, in one awful, terrifying yell, they surged forward.

33
The Seventeen

The army and people of Calridian looked on in horror as the horde was released. The horde swarmed at them in all directions. Meanwhile, the Seventeen made sure they stood in the correct spots around the ring of fire, which encircled the Gate of Fire. Cyna was in place, and right beside her was the dragon, Esmerelda. Going around the circle to the left, each spaced from the other, came Sigmon. Sigmon taking the place of the Wanderer. Then Rutu, then Felix alongside the stone form of Hawkins. Then Ogla, then, a black donosin. As the black donosin had come within range of the Bear's Heart they were able to speak and then able to understand their position assignments. After the donosin, came the trio of Crimson, the Bear's Heart, and Lord Kapel. Continuing to the right was another black donosin, then Shepherd Rowland followed by Sunbeam and Tagro. Completing the circle was King Malick and the third black donosin, closest to Esmeralda.

Each of the Seventeen was in place as instructed and spread around the ring. And between each of them were the brave soldiers of the Kingdom of Calridian. Only two soldiers deep in most places, who along with the Seventeen, created two thin circles of defense. The Seventeen and the soldiers stood outside and around the ring of fire. And between the ring and the gate were the approaching horde. To make matters worse, those close to the Bear's Heart's side of the ring of fire also had approaching wolves to worry about.

The wolves would come after the item that they thought belonged to them.

The call came up from down the line and was repeated all the way around the circle. "Spears! Ready your spears." Those that didn't have a spear at first, had one thrust into their grip, and the spears were lowered toward the flames as the horde approached. Lalatco and Leah stood in front of the Bear's Heart as the horde struck. But their initial surge was pushed back with ease as around the circle, these horde were feeling pain for perhaps the first time. Spears with the tips fashioned by Lumpkin and Cyna poked at the horde and the horde jumped back, unsure of this new development.

Three short blasts sounded on the trumpet as the dwarf still standing near the king sent short, loud, and crisp noises into the air. Lumpkin heard them loud and clear. He was standing right behind Cyna and urged her on. "Time. It is. Time."

Cyna closed her eyes. She held up Meslar's staff and began to recite the spell she had spent so much time learning over the last few days. With the pause in battle around her and the stalled horde, she was able to keep her attention on the spell. As she reached the end of the spell, the staff started vibrating in her hand and a rush of power ushered forth from it. A force like a wind encircled the ring of fire and the flames from the ring increased in height as a quick burst of blue lit the sky. Cyna stumbled a bit, shaking off the effects of the spell. But she had done it. One down and two to go.

All around the ring of fire, the people of Calridian sensed the change. Something was happening. They had no idea what the result would be. But it gave them a chance, a hope. The king smiled and thrust his fist in the air. The stone gargoyle had worked. Lord Kapel's positioning had worked. So far, they had held the horde back. They could do this!

Mit and his group, which had first retreated, stopped to watch how things would progress. The goblins watched in delight as their leader Bluey opened the Gate of Fire. That delight was quick to disappear, however, as they lost sight of him in the mass of the horde. Mit watched with curiosity as the horde started to advance and were repelled. Then all at once the height of the ring of fire changed. Something was happening, and Mit was on the outside looking in. A place he couldn't stand being. "Let's go," he yelled and charged back toward the ring.

The goblins were quick to follow him, eager to find out what had happened to their leader. The orcs followed as well, always one to follow the masses. But those from Castle Mystic wanted no part of whatever was about to occur, and they retreated.

Mit led the smaller group toward where he saw the young girl holding up the staff. A rag-tag group of goblins and orcs ran behind him. None of them knew what was going to happen, or why they were charging into this battle. Not even Mit knew what he would do now. He just had to be there.

The horde saw the flames rise higher in front of them, but they still knew what was on the other side. Painful weapons, but also freedom. Where they were was nothing. They needed, wanted, to be away from this place. This fire. So as one, they attacked again.

Lalatco and Leah were ready for them. They stepped forward each thrusting their spear forward with authority, impaling a horde on the end of their spears. The horde creatures cried out in pain and fell, but more of their brethren were right there. Lalatco and Leah pulled back their spears, and swung them wide, trying to keep the horde at bay. The soldiers of Calridian alongside Lalatco and Leah joined in the fight, mounting the defense.

Although the fire was not painful or unbearable in heat, it clouded the vision of both the horde and those of Calridian, making it a desperate fight. Lord Kapel from his spot, shouted out warnings when he could and struck out with his spear as a horde came in striking distance. Lalatco, Leah, and the others next to them managed to keep the horde busy. But they heard the all too familiar howls of wolves; they were about to strike.

The same chaotic fighting was happening all the way around the circle. Felix with his impressive speed was helping his side of the battle, as were the yixl. Rutu stayed in the required spot while Karth and Brigand worked in concert with the yixl to continue to oppose any surge from the horde. Brigand put his healing skill to work where he could and saved a few soldiers. The soldiers across from them were struggling. Sunbeam could do little against the horde, and Tagro was hard-pressed. Those warriors on that side of the battle stood on the edge of disaster. Shepherd Rowland saw it. Sensed it. Calling to the closest human soldier next to him he yelled. "Do not move from this spot!"

The man nodded, stepping into where Shepherd had been. The older man picked up a spear from a fallen soldier, and with a spear in each hand, stepped forward into the line. The spears swung around him in constant circles. Shepherd was a one-man wheel of pain. The spears never stopped moving nor did he. He paved his way through the line of horde, some falling and others running from this wheel of terror. He cleared the way from his previous spot all the way to Subeam and Tagro.

King Malick saw the destruction that Rowland caused and couldn't help but smile. The king returned his focus to those in front of him, any time a horde would threaten to break through, the king would extend his spear as long as his arms would allow, poking the horde and forcing them back. Off to his right, he saw Mit and goblins racing towards Cyna. But there was little the king could do. He had to stay in his spot. He struck another horde that broke through the line. This one didn't get up again.

Mit and the goblins and orcs started to scream as they charged toward their target. Cyna lost her focus and had to start over, struggling to concentrate amid all the chaos.

"You can do it," Lumpkin yelled. "Again, start, start again."

Cyna did as he said, closing her eyes again and restarting the spell. Cyna didn't see the battle around her where Elonda dropped to her knees avoiding a horde's reach, and Jyres came over the top plunging the spear tip right into the face of the horde. He backed away just enough, from a second horde who grazed him for just a moment. Jyres shook off the effects of the touch, waving it back with his spear.

"What do we do about the enemy at our backs?" yelled Elonda over the noise of battle.

Jyres didn't know how to answer her.

34
Desperation

alatco and Leah found a moment of calm in the battle and took a look behind them. The wolves were almost upon them. Lord Kapel nodded at the couple and turned to face the oncoming wolves. Crimson, on the other side of Lalatco, released a stream of fire at the wolves, which stalled their advance. Two wolves were completely engulfed by the dragon's flames and fell to the ground after a few agonizing moments. A few other wolves howled in pain as the fire licked at them. Leah and Lalatco were forced to turn back as the horde attacked again. The dwarf fighting next to Lalatco went down in a heap; a horde had sustained his hold on the dwarf long enough. Lalatco whipped his spear around and the horde felt its bite. A horde grabbed onto Leah, and she was in pain as soon as the contact started. But she pushed the spear into the horde's arm, and it lost its grip on her.

A roar from Crimson was heard over the sounds of battle, and Lalatco wondered how many wolves a dragon could fight at once. But then another roar sounded, not from a dragon, it was a different sound. And Lalatco heard it a second time.

"It is the Wanderer," called Lord Kapel. "And he has brought friends."

The Wanderer, riding a bear at the head of many running black donosin, was leading them against the enemy wolves. The bears roared and the wolves turned to meet their charge. The two groups collided. Teeth tore into bear flesh, as claws racked wolves' faces.

The Wanderer slashed down with his sword, holding on tight to his perch with his other hand. It was a ferocious battle, one that would not be easily won.

As the bears charged in, Cyna completed a second run through the spell. The flames around the ring rose even higher and started to curve inward now at the top of the flames. The blast of blue color filled the sky again as Cyna fell to her knees, the power the spell demanded sapping at her strength. Lumpkin was right next to her, helping her back up.

Esmeralda let loose a steady stream of fire at the approaching goblins and orcs. They all fell to the ground in an effort to avoid the blast. One failed to do so and was burnt to a crisp where he stood. "Kaleido, here now!" roared Esmeralda.

Kaleido responded right away, flying to the spot.

"This is your spot now," the older female dragon said. Then Esmeralda charged and pounced on the small army of goblins and orcs. Some had not even begun to move again before the dragon was amongst them. Esmeralda stomped on one and caught two more in another blast of fire. A flick of her tail sent another one flying. The orcs and goblins were running away faster than they had attacked. As much as they perhaps wanted to find Bluey, that desire paled in comparison to the need to get away from a dragon.

Mit, however, had survived the chaos, sneaking closer to where Cyna now stood. He hid behind a rock and watched as the dwarf, Lumpkin, handed her a vial of liquid, which she drank without question.

"Are you okay?" Jyres yelled to his sister.

Cyna turned to watch Jyres and Elonda battle horde after horde. "I am okay," she replied. One more time, she could do this. She nodded to Lumpkin, held out the staff with the glowing purple gem, and closed her eyes.

All around the Ring of the Seventeen defenses were growing thin, and the horde was taking its toll. Soldiers and horde alike lay motionless on the ground. More and more horde broke through the lines and the Seventeen began to be hard-pressed to stay on their spots. King Malick stole a quick glance over his shoulder. He could tell the delga, Cyna, was in the midst of her last spell. Somehow, they had to hang on, they were so close. Malick's spear moved with lightning speed as the horde drew closer to him. No one could breach his defenses. To his right, he saw the line breaking down, but Digmon came running over, trying to stem the tide.

When the bears attacked Lord Kapel, had sent Digmon over to help, but now he, too, would be hard-pressed. The only part of the circle that seemed to be in good shape was where the yixl, Felix, Karth, and Brigand were. The horde didn't even want to approach that side of the combat anymore. Seeing this, Karth sprinted around the fighting lines to support Sigmon. And Brigand raced over to his left to support Ogla and the soldiers there.

On the opposite side of the ring, Shepherd Rowland had held the lines well. But he was tiring fast. Tagro and the dwarves were helping him as much as possible. Shepherd, now with only one spear, thrust it at a horde, catching it in the shoulder. The horde shrank back, and Shepherd struck out again. But while the man was occupied a horde was able to get behind Shepherd. Before Tagro could even shout a warning, the horde had Shepherd in his grasp. A few moments later, the man fell to the ground, his life gone from him.

Lalatco, Leah, and Lord Kapel still stood tall, but many around them had fallen. They ducked and weaved and thrust their spears in return, doing all they could to hold onto the possibility of winning, as their chances of that grew smaller by the moment.

The Wanderer and the bears with him pressed the attack. The wolves were a determined enemy, but the brute strength of the bears was starting to turn the tide. The black donosin continued to push the wolves back and away from the ring of fire and the Bear's Heart. The bear the Wanderer was riding pounced on a wolf, crushing it with the weight of the bear. The Wanderer jumped from the back of the bear, landing on top of a wolf, impaling it with his sword. Three black donosin ran past him, slamming into the wolves nearby.

Jyres and Elonda fought with desperation now as those soldiers nearest to them had fallen to the horde's touch. The line was thinning. Not just here, but all along the circle. Jyres took a quick look around as Elonda swung her spear at the nearest horde. Out of the corner of his eye, he saw someone slinking in the shadows, moving toward Cyna. Jyres didn't even think, he just ran. He ran straight toward the person, unsure of who it was or what they were doing.

"Jyres," Elonda called, her voice one of panic. She would be outmatched without Jyres there to help. Elonda swung her spear in random, quick patterns. But it seemed to do little to slow the advance of the creatures. But from out of nowhere, something shattered in front of her, and beams of light shot out, blinding the horde for the time being. Elonda, although also affected by the potion, was happy that the dwarf alchemist had been paying attention.

Jyres approached Cyna's position just after the unknown person had arrived. This time Jyres could see who it was. There was no question, it was Mit. Mit had a short sword in his hand and was casting his gaze side to side as he approached the young delga. She was standing stone-still with her eyes closed and her voice giving life to the words of the spell. Mit took a half a step back when he saw Jyres staring at him. "No, this is not what it looks like!" Mit claimed. "Just," Mit stammered, unsure of what to say, or really how to put into words what he was thinking. But then he realized it didn't matter what he was going to say. Jyres charged him.

Mit brought his sword up to block Jyres's first swipe of the spear. Mit, who had never had a lot of practice with a blade, backed off as Jyres kept coming. "Jyres," he tried again. But he saw the look in the man's eyes. The eyes of a brother who had thought his sister was in danger. Was she in danger? What were his intentions?

Jyres attacked again and this time Mit almost lost his arm as he dodged the spear. Mit threw himself at Jyres, sword flailing. Jyres sidestepped him with ease and knocked him to the ground with the thick shaft of his spear. Mit hit the ground and dropped the sword. He scrambled toward the sword, but Jyres was faster, flicking it away with the end of his spear. Mit rolled onto his back, staring up into the eyes of the man he had dubbed the Hero of Heritage.

Jyres turned the spear end over end in his hands and whacked Mit in the side with the shaft of the spear. He was rewarded with a groan from the man on the ground. Jyres did it one more time, before turning the spear again, and holding the point at Mit's throat.

"Please, no," blurted Mit. "Please, I wasn't going to hurt her. No, please."

"You weren't?" said Jyres with a half grin. "Maybe, maybe not." Jyres shook his head and clenched his teeth. "Ahh"! A scream of rage ushered forth from Jyres. Then he lowered the spear. "But, lucky for you, you are not worth it." Jyres turned to walk away.

Mit blew out a sigh of relief. It was a short-lived feeling, however. He would not let Jyres come out on top again. Mit saw the sword lying to his right. In slow movements, he gathered the sword again, stood up, and charged.

Jyres had turned his back, looking to join the fight again, and didn't hear Mit charge. He was lucky that the dwarf Lumpkin was again paying attention to the battles around him and the dwarf shouted a warning. Jyres ducked down and pulled his spear in close, not sure at all where Mit was coming from.

Mit saw Jyres move and tried to adjust his charge. But he stumbled. Mit Merrituk stumbled right onto Jyres's spear.

Jyres stood. Shocked by the turn of events. Removing the spear from the dead body before him, he turned to get back to Elonda. He had no more time to spend on the man who was Mit Merrituk. Jyres ran back to Elonda and arrived just in time, for the horde had her encircled. Jyres stole a look at Cyna. *Come on*, he thought. *Finish the spell.*

Although it is rare, it is not so rare that Gargan himself hadn't warned Jyres of the possibility in their battles with Bram. It had happened on a few occasions in the history of the gargoyles. Gargan didn't know if it was a feeling of immediate danger or the feeling that his dear friend was in trouble. Whatever the reason, Gargan's stone exterior shattered. Gargan roared and then shielded his eyes from the bright sun. For the first time in his life, Gargan had awoken in the day. Gargan had only known of it happening to other gargoyles twice in his time, but here he was, awake.

He turned to see wolves retreating from the gate, with bears on their heels. Beyond that he saw the ring of fire, reaching so high into the sky. And although he couldn't make out the details, he knew that his friends were in the fight of their lives. This realization sparked something inside him. And he roared as loud as he had ever roared before. The sound filled the western side of the gate.

And all at once and all around him, his clan members were breaking out of their stone slumber. At least thirty gargoyles now awake, despite the sun, turned to their leader. "We need to take to the skies," he roared "Now!"

Those that had true wings and flying ability, helped those that did not, lifting them into the air high enough for them to be able to catch the air and glide upon the winds. Soon, they were all in the sky and racing towards the battle.

Cyna uttered the last words from her mouth and collapsed to the ground. A final burst of power leaped from her and the staff, flowing like a wave into the ring of fire. The ring of fire rose even higher and curved in even more. Soon the ring would completely close in on itself, one big dome of fire over the gate. A fantastic shade of blue once again flashed in the sky.

Every being and creature felt the power and heard the rush of fire as the spell to unmake the gate was completed. All signs of battle fell away as many turned to see what would happen now. The ring of fire became like a wall of impenetrable flame. The horde that were still on the inside of the ring could not pass through the flames now. Those that tried were met with an immeasurable force that blocked their way. The horde now screamed in unison, a wail of despair as they realized they were trapped.

But not all horde were on the inside, some were on the outside. The ones who had managed to break through the lines of the Calridians. Two were near Lord Kapel, who looked over his head and saw a stream of gargoyles. He looked at the flames reaching toward each other and knew what had to be done.

"Here," he yelled as loud as he could, hoping to get the attention of the gargoyles. "Here," he screamed again and saw two gargoyles swoop down his way.

As they did so, he dodged the touch of one horde and stuck his spear in the chest of a second. He pushed harder, and the point penetrated the gelatinous but resistant body that was the horde. Then, he tried to raise the horde as high as he could and looked directly at the gargoyles.

Gargan looked at the flames getting higher and higher and understood at once. He yelled, "Spears! Now!" to all his clan mates in the sky and then looked down as the second horde got ahold of Lord Kapel. Lalatco rushed to his aid, but it was too late. Gargan roared and swung down low. Holding out his hand, Lalatco tossed the spear to him. Gargan swooped to his right, impaling a horde as he flew by. Gargan rode the wind to the top of the flames. There he threw the spear, and spear and the horde went toppling over the flames and inside the wall that was closing all too fast.

The other gargoyles and the four dragons joined in the effort. Dragons and gargoyles alike swooped down, as the remaining Calridians threw them spears. At least twenty horde had broken the lines and remained on the outside of the wall of fire. But that number started to diminish, one after another, as the might and speed of the dragons and gargoyles were on full display. The few horde that realized what was going on made a break for it. Crimson speared another one and soared high to throw it over the flames as the others threatened to get away.

Kaleido snagged a running horde and roared with delight as he deposited it on the other side. All eyes darted around looking for any more horde as the flames were about to reach each other and complete the dome of fire over the gate.

The king was about to breathe a sigh of relief when his eyes fell on a retreating horde. "There, there!" he screamed. He saw a gargoyle rushing over him and he threw his spear in the air. Gargan caught it and raced on.

Jyres's eyes tracked the gliding gargoyle as it neared its prey. He turned back to the ring of fire. "He's not going to make it," Jyres warned.

"Yes, he will," Elonda said next to him. "He can do it."

Both Elonda and Jyres trained their eyes upward as Gargan raced toward the top of the fire with an impaled horde dangling underneath him. "Come on," pleaded Jyres.

Gargan flew straight up the fire parallel to him. He curved with the fire, reaching the top. He threw the spear forward as the fire reached for each other. The horde screamed one final time as he fell into the smallest opening as the fire closed the dome.

Cheers went up from the Calridians after Gargan deposited the last of the horde inside the dome of fire. Elonda and Jyres wrapped each other in a hug. Lalatco kissed Leah, and the cheers grew in strength. Then the dome of fire started to pulse in alternating bursts of blue and orange. A burning and crackling sound of increasing strength soon followed the pulsing. As fast as the cheers had come, they dissipated faster, as the surviving Calridians tried to get away from whatever was happening inside the dome. Gargoyles landed, helping to carry the wounded or dead and everyone helped the Calridian or body next to them. No one would be left behind.

Jyres turned, with frantic motions, looking for his sister. He saw Lumpkin, kneeling next to her. He ran to them, sliding down beside them. "Is she okay?" he stammered.

"Breathing, breathing," the dwarf said.

Jyres nodded and scooped her up in his arms and they ran away from the dome of fire. The noise increased to a deafening crackling as if the whole land was on fire. And then there was absolute silence...Before an enormous eruption of sound, wind, and energy. Jyres was knocked from his feet with the force, sending him and Cyna tumbling to the ground. Calridians were experiencing the same effect all around the battlefield. Jyres turned his face to see the fire flowing out in all directions. He had to shield his eyes from the wind and light. And then...all at once...it was over.

As the smoke cleared, Jyres scanned the area. No ring of fire, no Gate of Fire, no horde. Gone. It was all gone.

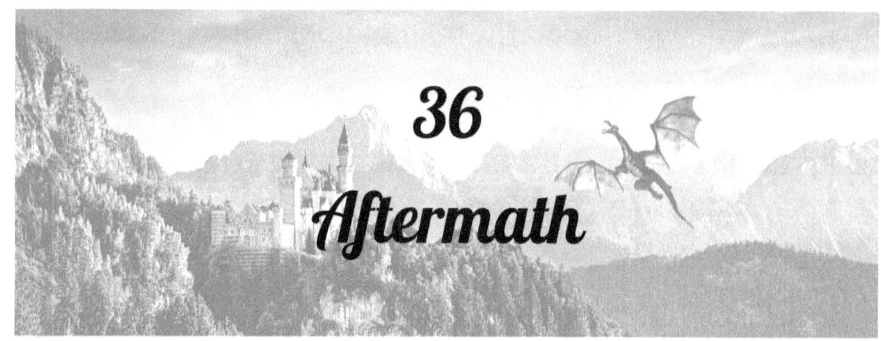

36
Aftermath

All survivors stayed on the ground for a moment, looking back in awe at the now-empty area. They had done it, the horde was gone. Jyres turned toward the girl in his arms. Her eyes remained closed, but he could feel her body inhaling and exhaling in his arms. With care, he set her down on the ground.

"Cyna," he called to her. After getting no response he tried again. "Cyna, come on Sis." He started to worry now. Why wouldn't she wake up?

Again no response. Jyres looked around him as the Calridians started to gather together in groups. He saw someone walking among them from group to group and realized it was Brigand. "Brigand," he called. "Over here, please!" Jyres pleaded.

The former knight came over right away. Kneeling by the girl, he started to look her over. Jyres tried to stay patient as he took in the delga next to him. Brigand looked haggard. But Jyres supposed they all did. He watched as Brigand reached down and put his hand on her forehead. Brigand took a deep breath and then a moment later, Cyna's eyes fluttered open.

"Cyna," Jyres breathed. "Cyna, it's me, you're okay."

"Brother," she said in a weak voice.

Jyres turned to Brigand, nodding his thanks, and the former knight sat back, exhausted. Turning back to Cyna he said, "It will be okay."

"What happened?"

"You did it," Jyres said, still trying to believe it himself. "You did it. You saved us all."

Cyna smiled at him and Jyres reached down and pulled her close. Elonda dropped down and embraced them. They stayed that way, granting each other comfort. A few moments later they stood up, Jyres still holding the now-sleeping Cyna. They were greeted as soon as they did so with hugs and smiles from Leah and Lalatco.

King Malick called to everyone and they started to gather around him. As they did so, he breathed a weary sigh. They had won. But the victory came with costs. The king scanned the battlefield. Too many bodies lay motionless. Many Calridians had fallen, including Shepherd Rowland and Lord Kapel. And of course, Vurth and Demorous the Fierce. He also noticed the many stone gargoyles who returned to their rock-like state as soon as the gate and everything with it disappeared.

Malick saw Jyres, Elonda, and Cyna join the group. The young girl was still cradled in his arms. And right behind them were Lalatco and Leah. Malick nodded in their direction and then began speaking. "Citizens of Calridian. What we did here today saved the kingdom. Together we have rid this kingdom of the horde forever! Against all odds, we have done it. But it was not without loss. Many fell here today and gave their lives so that the rest of us would be safe. They will be remembered forever."

The king paused, lowering his head, and the others around him followed suit, sharing a moment of silence for those who gave everything for everyone else. After a bit of time had passed, the king began again. "We will bring all those who gave their lives today back with us to Castle Serenity, and a fitting memorial will be built in their honor." Malick looked over the gathered group, making eye contact with many of them. "But it is also a day to celebrate. We earned this victory. Every one of us. And I, the King of Calridian, thank you from the bottom of my heart. Well done, all of you."

A few cheers went up from among the group, but overall it was a somber and exhausted group. Celebration would have to come later.

A celebration and memorial were held many days later at the Valley of the Dragons. The valley was packed with citizens of Calridian. Esmerlada led the gathered assembly to the western side of the valley. A cemetery had been placed there with headstones for everyone who had lost their life in the epic battle around the ring of fire. In the middle of the area stood Vurth. The body of Vurth, forever encased in stone. Malick said a few words and then the many who were gathered walked among the headstones, many stopping and spending a moment with their lost loved one. Although they did not have his body, a headstone was there for Demorous as well. Right next to Vurth.

The Wanderer, with the Bear's Heart at his hip, stood in front of Lord Kapel's marker which was not far from the stature of Vurth and Demorous's stone. Two black donosin were with him and they talked in quiet tones with each other. Next to them, were a pair of humans, standing in front of Shepherd Rowland's headstone.

Sometime later, the crowd moved on, heading back toward the castle. Jyres, Elonda, Cyna, Lalatco, Leah, and Gargan remained behind and gathered in the middle of the site, in front of Vurth. They all stood there in silence, each lost in their own thoughts and memories of their friend. A long while went by before anyone spoke. Jyres, sensing it was the right time, was the one to break the silence.

"Vurth was one of a kind. And now that we have shared this moment, you know there is only one thing left to do. And that is what Vurth would want us to do."

"Which is?" said Elonda with a smile.

Then in unison, they all said. "Celebrate."

Which they did.

Epilogue

A lmost a year had gone by since the great battle around the Gate of Fire and Lalatco and Jyres were together in Lalatco's and Leah's home in the Malkin Forest.

"It has been a while," said Lalatco, with nervousness in his voice.

"No need to worry, I am sure everything is fine," Jyres replied.

The comment seemed to do little to help the elf, who began pacing the room. Jyres smiled to himself, finding it to be very endearing. Lalatco didn't have to pace very long. A knock on the door, and the door flew open. Cyna was standing there, a wide smile on her face.

"Well?" said Lalatco.

"It's a boy!" shouted Cyna. "And Leah and baby are doing wonderful."

Lalatco's relief was evident but he was soon overwhelmed with joy. He hugged Jyres before running for the door. He stopped and looked back. "Are you coming?"

Jyres smiled. "I will be right there."

Cyna stepped back as the elf hurried out the door to go meet his son. "Well, he is happy," said the young delga wizard.

"He should be. I am happy for them both."

"King Malick says it is a sign. The birth of this baby is the first offspring from a human and an elf in hundreds of years."

Jyres smiled at his sister. "So, you have heard that as well, have you? Yes, I think it is a sign. Our past is behind us. The Kingdom of

Calridian is thriving and a new race has just entered the world. It is a good day."

"What are the chances?" Cyna asked.

"What are the chances of what?" Jyres replied, unsure of what Cyna was saying.

"That Lalatco and Leah would have a baby just two days before you and Elonda would be married."

The thought of being married to Elonda and that it was only two days away brought a huge smile to Jyres's face. As Jyres thought back on all that had happened, all that he had been through, he couldn't help but shake his head and smile. To come out of all of that with lifelong friends, a sister, and the love of his life was something that would have been unfathomable for the young man who had left his village in search of a better life for his people. But here he was.

He looked over to his sister, all smiles by the door. "Chances? I don't know," he said. "Some will say it was fate that I went to that first meeting of the week of peace, some will say it was all prophesied." He shook his head and smiled yet again. "What I do know is that we could not have done it without each other. All of us, together. Now, let's go meet that baby and congratulate our friends."

"Our family," Cyna corrected.

"Our family," Jyres agreed.

THE END

About the author

The Ring of the Seventeen is B.J. Vanderhoof's third novel and the final novel of the Gate of Fire Series. His love for fantasy and science fiction inspired him to begin writing. When he is not writing, Vanderhoof is working at a YMCA as an Associate Executive. He enjoys playing board games, watching movies, reading, and spending time with family. Vanderhoof lives with his wife and three children in Appleton, Wisconsin. Visit his website at https://bjvanderhoof.com

Acknowledgements

It is complete! The Gate of Fire Series is finished. It has been an absolute joy to write this series and I sincerely hope that you, the reader, enjoyed the journey. I would not be able to continue writing and publishing without the support of my readers. Thank you so much for coming along with me on my writing adventures.

There is a lot of work that goes into both writing and publication. It takes a lot of people to bring a book to life, and I wouldn't be a self-published author without the time and talents of many others. First, a special thank you to my father who was the initial editor. Just like in book 2, he helped me a great deal in catching all those silly mistakes and correcting things that didn't fit. He always seemed to know what paragraph needed that one specific word. I would also like to thank Belle Manuel for her excellent editing. She was the editor for both The Keepers of the Key and The Ring of the Seventeen and I couldn't be happier with her work.

Every self-published author needs a great-looking book cover to draw the attention of potential readers. Morgan Johnson made sure that I had a great-looking book. Morgan did the cover art for this book and The Keepers of the Key. Thank you, Morgan, for your hard work and for your ability to bring the images in my head to life.

I also want to take a moment to remember my Grandpa. Gramps was one of a kind, and I miss him every day. My Grandpa was also my Godfather and was one of the most influential people in my life. Many of my readers knew and loved my Grandpa, as well. Each one of us perhaps remembers different things that we hold close. For me, I remember his love for God, his love for his family, and his humor. Each one of the books of the Gate of Fire Series contains a classic Gramps saying or phrase. I expect that some of my readers picked up on some of those classic quotes. Books one and two each contained one such phrase, and this book had two such entries. These quotes from my Grandpa in books two and three were spoken by Vurth. He is a character whose humor developed throughout the series and I hope he was a character who made many of my readers smile while reading and remembering Gramps.

In a very unplanned and seemingly impossible turn of events, one of my best friends and I published our first book at almost the same time. And again, it happened with book two. And somehow again with book 3, we were only a couple of months apart. Throughout the process of writing and publishing, we urged each other on. Knowing there was another person out there battling the same struggles, overcoming hurdles, and at last achieving lifelong goals was essential to the writing process. Encouragement to complete the task was naturally born as you saw your lifelong friend complete another step in the journey. This friendly competition was welcome and needed. Thank you, Ryan Johnson, for your friendship and inspiration, and best of luck on your next book. I can't wait to read it.

A special THANK YOU to these wonderful Kickstarter Supporters

Greg Schmidt
Michael Washburn
Ellen Pilcher
Brian Cretzmeyer
Justin Vanderhoof
Justin
Nick Simmons
Debra ann Wilson
Collin J. Vanderhoof
Andrea Cox
Jason "Coach" Daily
Christopher Smith
Joshua Vick
Mom and Dad